D1006507

CALGARY PUBLIC LIBRARY

SEP — ⌐ 2012

SPOOKYGIRL:
paranormal investigator

SPOOKYGIRL:
paranormal investigator

JILL BAGUCHINSKY

DUTTON BOOKS

A member of Penguin Group (USA) Inc.

DUTTON B OOKS
A member of Penguin Group (USA) Inc.
Published by the Penguin Group
Penguin Group (USA) Inc., 375 Hudson Street, New York, New York 10014, U.S.A.
Penguin Group (Canada), 90 Eglinton Avenue East, Suite 700, Toronto, Ontario, Canada M4P 2Y3
(a division of Pearson Penguin Canada Inc.)
Penguin Books Ltd, 80 Strand, London WC2R 0RL, England
Penguin Ireland, 25 St Stephen's Green, Dublin 2, Ireland (a division of Penguin Books Ltd)
Penguin Group (Australia), 250 Camberwell Road, Camberwell, Victoria 3124, Australia
(a division of Pearson Australia Group Pty Ltd)
Penguin Books India Pvt Ltd, 11 Community Centre, Panchsheel Park, New Delhi 110017, India
Penguin Group (NZ), 67 Apollo Drive, Rosedale, Auckland 0632, New Zealand
(a division of Pearson New Zealand Ltd.)
Penguin Books (South Africa) (Pty) Ltd, 24 Sturdee Avenue, Rosebank, Johannesburg 2196, South Africa
Penguin Books Ltd, Registered Offices: 80 Strand, London WC2R 0RL, England

This book is a work of fiction. Names, characters, places, and incidents are either the product of the
author's imagination or are used fictitiously, and any resemblance to actual persons, living or dead,
business establishments, events, or locales is entirely coincidental.

Copyright © 2012 by Jill Baguchinsky

All rights reserved. No part of this publication may be reproduced or transmitted in any form or by any
means, electronic or mechanical, including photocopying, recording, or any information storage and
retrieval system now known or to be invented, without permission in writing from the publisher, except
by a reviewer who wishes to quote brief passages in connection with a review written for inclusion in a
magazine, newspaper, or broadcast.

The publisher does not have any control over and does not assume any responsibility for author
or third-party websites or their content.

LIBRARY OF CONGRESS CATALOGING-IN-PUBLICATION DATA

Baguchinsky, Jill.
Spookygirl : paranormal investigator / by Jill Baguchinsky.—1st ed.
p. cm.
Summary: "Fifteen-year-old Violet can see ghosts and communicate with
the dead, so it's up to her to uncover the truth behind the school's
paranormal activity and to finish the investigation that led to her
mother's untimely death."—Provided by publisher.
ISBN 978-0-525-42584-7 (hardcover)
[1. Psychic ability—Fiction. 2. Mothers—Fiction. 3. Dead—Fiction.
4.High schools—Fiction. 5. Schools—Fiction.] I. Title.
PZ7.B14215Spo 2012
[Fic]—dc23
2011052673

Published in the United States by Dutton Books, a member of Penguin Group (USA) Inc.
345 Hudson Street, New York, New York 10014
www.penguin.com/teen

Designed by Jeanine Henderson
Set in Adobe Caslon

Printed in USA First Edition

1 3 5 7 9 10 8 6 4 2

For Rhonda,
my favorite Time Lady,
who knows a thing or two about being spooky

SPOOKYGIRL:
paranormal investigator

CHAPTER ONE
death, high school, and other necessary evils

I was sitting in the Tranquility Room with my sketchbook and Mrs. Morris—nice, quiet, unobtrusive Mrs. Morris—when I heard the clang. Although it was muffled, it was still loud enough to startle me into dropping my charcoal, which rolled to a stop near the casket stand. Before I could pick it up, Dad's voice called out from the embalming room at the rear of the building.

"Violet? Can you help me?" He sounded more than a little frazzled.

Crap. So much for an uninterrupted art session.

Leaving the sketchbook on a chair, I hurried down the hall through Dad's office and the prep room. Dad stood in the embalming room's doorway, holding a tube and a container of who-knows-what liquid.

"Someone's in there with me," he said, and his remark was punctuated by an instrument tray zipping through the air and smacking against the door frame, inches from his head. The collision produced a second loud clang, and the now-dented tray toppled to the floor, where another tray already rested.

Not again.

"Yeah, that's kind of obvious. I'll handle it." I ducked past him into the room. I'm not even supposed to be in the embalming room—I'm fifteen years old, so obviously I'm unlicensed—but sometimes dealing with the dead means having to break a few rules.

The room was utilitarian—neat and cold and stark, with hospital lighting and supply shelves lining the walls. One wall had a big door that led to the freezer. The naked body of an old man with thinning curly hair lay on a table in the center of the room, his lower regions covered with a sheet. Aside from some scattered implements, everything looked orderly and clean—but apparently the old man thought it wasn't clean enough. Yeah, he was dead on the table, waiting to be embalmed, but he also stood in the middle of the room, translucent and blue and kind of shimmery, dressed in dark coveralls. He was muttering to himself and scrubbing the bare cement floor with a ghostly mop; his stooped posture caused a few limp gray curls to fall over his forehead, partly veiling his intense, slightly crazy gaze. He looked like a character in a horror movie, probably one with a really low budget.

Ugh. Confused newbies are such a pain.

"Excuse me? Sir?" I tried to sound polite instead of bored; this kind of thing really gets old after a while.

He didn't even look up. "Scat, missy. Can't you see I'm working? This floor won't clean itself."

"You don't have to do that."

"It's my job, ain't it?" He finally glanced at me, his jaw jutting forward in defiance. "You tell that man in the white coat to stop getting in my way and making a mess with those chemicals, or I'll throw something else at him. And this time I won't miss."

I glanced back at Dad, who was watching me with a puzzled look. He couldn't see or hear the old man's ghost. "Mister?" I said, trying again with the old grump. "You do know you're dead, right?"

The man scrubbed, then paused, then scrubbed a little more, then stopped again and looked at his body on the table. "Dead?"

"Yeah. You remember?"

He held up his hand in front of his eyes, flexing his fingers experimentally. "Dead."

"That's right."

"Well, that'd explain why I can see right through my dadgum hand, wouldn't it?"

"Yep. It would."

"But I feel pretty good." He leaned the mop against the embalming table—it disappeared as soon as he let it go, but he didn't seem to notice—and did an awkward little jig. "My knees don't even hurt anymore. And the chest pains are gone."

"That's how it works." I stepped a little closer; now I could read the name patch on his coveralls. HENRY.

"So what now?" he asked.

"Now you move on." It seemed pretty obvious to me. Most newbies figure these things out for themselves, and they go off on their own. Some of them haunt their favorite hangouts or their least favorite relatives; others just go on to . . . well, wherever ghosts go. Into the light or whatever. I don't know. I don't really care. I just get tired of having to explain these things every time a recently deceased person throws a fit. The only interesting ghosts are those with unfinished business; Henry was just a boring, run-of-the-mill dead guy.

"Where do I go?" he asked.

"The afterlife?" I shoved my black bangs out of my eyes. "Look, I'm sorry, but I don't know the details, okay? You're going to have to follow your instinct on this. Do you have a wife who died? Or a relative? Maybe they'll find you and help."

"Yeah, I had a wife. Died ten years ago." His tone was less than enthusiastic.

"Then you can go join her now."

"And go back to her nagging? For all eternity? No thanks."

"Well, you don't have to cross over, but you can't stay here."

He frowned as he considered his options, his bushy brows lowering to shadow his pale blue eyes. "Say, can I go back to work?"

"Um, I guess. As long as you don't think you work here."

"Of course I don't work here." He gave me a glare. "You think I'm slow or something? I'm a janitor for the Palmetto County school system. Forty-five years of dependable service."

"And going back to that is better than moving on?"

Henry wagged a finger at me. "You never met my Delores. I'd rather scrub toilets for another thousand years than hear her complaining again. So I can just . . . go?"

A ghost with issues might have been tied to a particular location, forced to haunt the place he died, but Henry didn't seem to have any such complications.

I nodded.

"Huh. Thanks, missy. You're okay." Whistling an off-key tune, he marched through the doorway—right through Dad—and down the hall toward the front entrance.

I followed just long enough to make sure he passed through the front door as well; then I went back to Dad. "He's gone."

"It was this guy?" Dad took a few steps toward the body. "Henry Boyd?"

"Yeah, it was good ol' Henry. He thought he was supposed to be cleaning, and you were getting in his way. Good thing I'll be around all the time now to handle stuff like this, huh?"

I'd been shuttled back and forth between Dad (on weekends) and Aunt Thelma (on weekdays) since I was eight. Dad had always said I'd live with him again once he took over the funeral home. When he finally bought the place a few months ago, the first thing he did was clear out his apartment's tiny second bedroom for me.

"This stuff doesn't really happen when you're not around," he said. I knew what he meant, unfortunately. Some ghosts tend to get more agitated when there's someone nearby who might actually be able to hear them. It gets them all excited, and it can be really inconvenient.

"Well, you'd better get used to it, because I'm not going anywhere." I grinned at him. More time with Aunt

Thelma just wasn't an option. I wouldn't put up with her anymore, and I knew Dad wouldn't, either. He was glad to have me around, even if it meant dealing with a weird mix of single-parent angst and unsettled spooks.

"Wouldn't have it any other way, kiddo. Okay, I shouldn't be too much longer in here, and then I'll have to get ready for Mrs. Morris's service."

"I'll keep her company until then."

Dad's eyes widened a little. "She's not haunting the place, too, is she?"

"Nah." Most ghosts move on before their bodies even make it to the funeral home. Only the confused ones stay close to their corpses. "But if I see her, I'll tell her you said hi."

"Great." Dad didn't look like he thought the idea was so great at all as he closed the door to the embalming room.

I went back to sketching Mrs. Morris in the Tranquility Room, which is where our in-house viewings and services are held. "Sorry to keep you waiting," I said as I sat back down next to her casket with my sketchbook. I was drawing her portrait to practice facial proportions.

Hey, dead bodies make good models, okay? Living models want to talk and move and stuff; dead ones are peaceful and still. I know it's called *life* drawing, but whatever.

After a while I heard Dad go upstairs to our apartment to shower and change; I kept right on working.

Yeah, Dad owns Addison Funeral Services, and we live in the apartment upstairs. Whenever I'm coming or going, I pass through the mortuary's formal front parlor, which is always full of flower arrangements and smells like wilting carnations. The Tranquility Room opens off the parlor, and the showcase room with all the sample coffins is just down the hall. Dad's office, a storage room, the prep room, and the embalming facility and freezer are at the back of the building, so it's not like you're parading past a pile of corpses whenever you're coming or going. Still, I can see how it might seem a little freaky.

It doesn't bother me, though. I'm used to dead people. They won't leave me alone. But even being confronted by the grumpiest dead person beats being around Aunt Thelma. She stepped in and helped raise me after my mom died, but she's strict and judgmental and I don't like her. Staying with her half the time while Dad went back to school and got his business going . . . Well, I understood why he needed help for a while, even if I didn't like it.

So now I eat and sleep and do my homework upstairs, while downstairs there are bodies in the freezer. It's as weird as it sounds, I guess, but I like helping Dad with his business, and he could really use the assistance. He lets me do stuff like hair and makeup—or as he sometimes calls it "death spackle," since it looks so fake and slathered on when it's not done right.

I do it right. I'd kept Mrs. Morris's makeup light, using just enough base to camouflage the chalky pallor of her skin. With her cheeks a little pink and wisps of white hair resting on her forehead, she looked like she'd just stretched out for a nap in her coffin.

It wasn't such a crazy idea. Her family had sprung for an Eternal Rest 3500. You can't find a better coffin without getting something custom made. Upholstered silk interior, padded with goose down . . . It's comfy. I know. I've tried it out.

I was finishing my sketch when Dad came back down. "Is she being an agreeable model?" he asked, walking up to do his final prefuneral check. Dad didn't really get my artistic new hobby, but he humored me about it. "You did a great job with her death spackle. Keep that up and you'll have a career waiting for you."

It's true. People are always dying, so there would always be a market—not that I wanted to spend my life decorating the dead. I had other plans—plans Dad didn't even know about. Still, I preened a little at the compliment. "She looks peaceful, doesn't she?"

"Peaceful, sure. But I had to sew her mouth shut and

use eye caps to get her that way." Eye caps are like huge contact lenses with little spikes; Dad puts them under corpses' eyelids to keep them closed.

I added a few delicate charcoal curls along the portrait's hairline. "I'm sure she didn't mind."

"If she did, she didn't complain." He grinned a little under his neat salt-and-pepper beard. "Almost done? I'm not sure how Mrs. Morris's relatives would feel about her being an art project."

I closed the sketchbook. "All done."

"Great. Oh, I was looking at the list your school sent earlier—"

Ugh. And just like that, my mood crashed down a little. "Don't remind me about school."

He ignored my complaining. "I'm not sure we got you enough shirts. And are you sure you don't want a backpack? You'll have lots of books to carry."

"I already told you. Mom's messenger bag will be fine." Purple with a lavender flower appliqué, it was the same beat-up old bag I'd used for years. It was one of only a handful of my mother's things that I had. Dad thought it wasn't big or sturdy enough to be a proper book bag, and he swore the shoulder strap was about to snap, but I knew he was wrong. Mom made it herself, and because of that, I knew it was strong enough to last.

"You might want something bigger, though."

"I used it last year at Lakewood. It was big enough." I'd stayed with Aunt Thelma so often last year that I'd been registered in her school district. Living full-time with Dad put me in a different district, so I would be transferring to Palmetto High for my sophomore year.

"Okay. But let me know if you change your mind. Anyway, Mrs. Morris is the only service scheduled for today, so I'll be free this evening. How about we go out, grab some dinner, and pick up those shirts?"

Palmetto High maintained a pretty strict dress code; as a result of Dad's overzealous single-parent nerves, I already owned enough plain white collared shirts and khaki pants to last me for three weeks without doing laundry. Then again, if buying another week's worth of shirts would make him stop worrying a little, I was okay with that. "Sounds good."

"Great." Dad smiled again. "I should finish getting things ready in here. I think it's time for you to go upstairs and—"

"Keep Buster out of trouble. I know." Babysitting Buster was the other part of my job at Addison Funeral Services.

"Thanks for your help, kiddo," Dad called as I went upstairs.

The apartment over the funeral home was teeny. The size made sense for a man living on his own, but it was pretty ridiculous for a father and daughter. The two bedrooms were practically microscopic; Dad had been using the second as an office, but he carted his computer and filing cabinets downstairs when I moved in. I didn't really mind the cramped space—I would've gladly slept on a couch in the living room, or even downstairs in one of the display coffins, if it meant more time with Dad.

I put my sketchbook and charcoal in the dresser drawer where I kept my art supplies, then went back to the living room and looked around. "Buster!"

A squeaky howl echoed from my dad's bedroom. I followed the sound and called Buster's name again when I reached the bedroom doorway.

The air in the room was at least twenty degrees colder than in the rest of the apartment. The sliding door to Dad's tiny closet was open; his neckties were floating and writhing in a circle near the bed, like a collection of airborne snakes in muted, mortician-appropriate colors. A nervous, giddy squeal emanated from nowhere apparent, causing the ties to shudder in midair.

Oh, Buster was definitely here.

"What are you doing, Buster?" Trying to sound as authoritative as possible, I grabbed for the nearest tie. It whipped away, the imitation silk brushing my fingertips.

Buster's taunting, wordless cries seemed to pulse from the walls themselves; it was impossible to tell exactly where he was. To tell the truth, it was impossible even to tell *what* he was. I've never been able to figure it out, so I've always thought of him as a poltergeist. An abnormal one. He does poltergeisty things, like making noises or knocking stuff around, but real poltergeists are more like pockets of built-up negative energy. They're not usually actual ghosts like Buster. He followed Mom home from an investigation like a stray dog when I was two and has just stuck around ever since. After Mom died, I let him follow me to Aunt Thelma's, but after he smashed her favorite casserole dish—an accident *I* got blamed for, since Aunt Thelma insists I make up all my ghost stuff for attention—I told him to stay with Dad instead. Buster's pretty good about obeying orders when he knows I mean business.

Well, most of the time.

He made a trembling shriek that sounded almost like a giggle, and the ties began to knot themselves together.

"You know how mad Dad's going to get if he sees this," I warned, stepping into the middle of the drifting circle of knotted ties. I reached for one again; this time I managed to get a grip before Buster could yank it away. Trying to pull it down was like being in a vertical tug-of-war with a linebacker. When the tie jerked upward and threatened to take me with it, I let go.

I didn't mind letting Buster have a little fun, but Mrs. Morris's guests would be arriving downstairs within minutes, and it wouldn't do to have an abnormal poltergeist banging around overhead during a funeral service. In the same tone I would've used on a misbehaving dog, I yelled, "BUSTER! BAD BOY!"

Buster's mischievous chortles turned into an anguished scream; he hated being scolded. The ties wadded themselves into a polyester ball and flopped down on my head. Wrinkled, knotted neckties hung off my shoulders and arms like ropes of seaweed off a swamp monster.

"CRATE, BUSTER. NOW!" I pointed toward the small, open trunk that sat in the apartment's tiny living room. The cold air left the room in a whoosh that knocked several of the ties off of me, and the trunk slammed shut. A hurt, angry whimper chastised me from inside.

"Sorry," I said, "but you know the rules. I'll let you out as soon as the service is over." I took a U-shaped piece of polished stone—obsidian—from a nearby shelf and slid it through the hole on the trunk's latch where a lock would normally go. Obsidian was supposed to be good for controlling misbehaving spirits. I wasn't sure why it worked, but it would keep him locked up until I set him free. With that taken care of, I gathered Dad's ties, unknotted them, and hung them back in the closet. Except for the occasional light thump as the trunk rocked back against the wall, Buster was quiet and calm.

Buster's not really such a bad ghost. Like a puppy, he just gets a little crazy sometimes if we're not strict enough with him. In his own ghostly way, I think he loves us. Mom was his favorite—she was the one who crate trained him—but he seems pretty attached to me, too. "He knows you're like your mom," Dad would say when Buster happily squawked at the sight of me or levitated one of his favorite toys in my direction. "He's much more active when you're around."

Muted noises carried up from downstairs. Car doors slammed outside; the front door opened and closed; voices droned too quietly for me to hear what was being said. For the next two hours or so—or longer, if Mrs. Morris had lots of friends who wanted to pay their respects during the viewing before the service—I had to tread lightly. Sound traveled too well through the old building; improving the soundproofing between the apartment and the funeral home was high on Dad's list of things to do, a list he often threatened to rename "Things That'll Never Get Done."

The sound restriction always made me a little stir-crazy. I couldn't watch TV, and I couldn't listen to music unless I used headphones. Hoping for a distraction, I browsed the bookshelves in the living room. My paperbacks were mixed in with Dad's textbooks and reference books from when he'd gone back to school for his mortuary science degree. That was a few months after Mom died, once the police investigation into her death ended and no charges were filed against Dad.

Aunt Thelma, of course, disapproved of her kid brother's career change. (In fact, she disapproved of everything.) They never discussed it in front of me, but I had eavesdropped on plenty of their conversations over the years. Aunt Thelma nagged him a lot.

"And what happened to being a doctor?"

"You know I gave that up years ago."

"When you met Robin and decided to be a ghost hunter." No one could drizzle their words with disdain quite like Aunt Thelma.

"I was struggling with my internship before I met Robin." Dad's voice always sounded soft and weary when Aunt Thelma brought up my mom.

"You can still go back to medical school," Aunt Thelma urged. "Take more classes. Try again."

"It wasn't right for me."

"Oh, and ghost hunting was?"

"Paranormal investigation, Thelma."

"At least you outgrew that. But funerals? Is this what you want to do with your life? Spend all day looking at dead bodies?"

"Maybe it is." I knew what he was saying—at least these dead people would stay dead. For the most part. Even though he couldn't sense ghosts the way Mom had, he'd had enough of them.

"A little girl shouldn't grow up surrounded by the dead."

"That's why I need you to help me with Violet for a little while. It'll be a tough couple of years—I'll have to go to school, get an apprenticeship, establish myself in the field. I can't do all that and take good care of her, too." Dad's voice had sounded rough and choked when he'd said that.

"She's like her mother," Aunt Thelma replied. The way she said it made it sound like there was something wrong with me. Ever since then, I'd always hated her a little.

I had already flipped through most of Dad's mortuary reference books over the summer, and it was hard to find my own books among all the clutter on the shelves. Originally Dad and I had attempted to keep our books separate, but after Buster threw everything around a few times, we stopped trying to sort through the volumes and just piled them back on the shelves instead.

It took me a good five minutes to locate what I was looking for—Mom's battered copy of *Wuthering Heights*, her favorite novel. I grabbed it not for the story, but for the treasure hidden inside—a faded business card for Palmetto Paranormal, the investigation business Mom and Dad had run together before her death. I'd just found the card tucked in the book a few months ago, soon after I'd moved in. It was plain, just black type on white card stock that had yellowed over time, with a generic logo, Mom's name, and the business's phone number and e-mail address.

That was what I wanted someday—a business like Palmetto Paranormal. Maybe it'd be easier to deal with this ghost stuff if I could turn it into something more interesting. A little excitement would be a good trade-off for having to review the whole ghost how-to manual with every newbie that came my way.

I hadn't told Dad yet about my plan, but I doubted he'd be too enthusiastic about it. He didn't even know I'd found Mom's card; he never talked about Palmetto Paranormal.

Nothing else on the shelves caught my interest, so I gave up and curled up on Dad's secondhand brown corduroy couch.

At this time tomorrow, the first day of school would be over. I couldn't ignore the ball of lead lurching in my stomach any longer.

For most of the summer, I'd been able to ignore my impending doom at Palmetto High. Spending so much time with Dad had been a welcome distraction, and I'd tricked myself into believing that the start of the school year was further away than it really was. There was no more denying it, though—my personal doomsday countdown had begun; school was less than eighteen hours away.

Last year at Lakewood had been bad enough. Lakewood High was small and exclusive; I hadn't had any friends, but I managed to blend in and be ignored. At least it was far enough away from Palmetto Crossing that no one knew my reputation. Back here people still remembered. They knew me. I was that weird girl whose dad killed her mom and got away with it. I was that girl who lived in a funeral home. I'd already heard a few comments at the mall food court the week before. And that was without them knowing my other little secret. You know, the whole ghost thing.

Then again, was it so bad to be weird? What happened to my mom was no one else's business. And living above a funeral home is a lot more interesting than living in the same kind of boring, Florida-style, pastel-colored single family home as everyone else in town. Plus, I was tired of downplaying the whole talking-to-ghosts thing. Ever since I'd moved back in with Dad full-time and found Mom's business card, I'd felt compelled to step up and own that part of my life, just like she had.

After all, if you're going to be a freak, you might as

well really be a *FREAK*, right? I'd spent too many years pretending to be normal, and all it had given me was the realization that normal was totally boring.

So why was my stomach still knotting up like a couple of Dad's ties at the mercy of Buster?

After Mrs. Morris's service ended and Dad got home from transporting the body to the cemetery, he changed from his tailored, somber, funeral-director-appropriate suit into a "Han shot first" *Star Wars* T-shirt over jeans, and we went out to dinner. When my dad wasn't busy with dead people, he was busy being a very big geek.

We went to Mama Chen's, a small, slightly dingy Chinese restaurant where I'd found a dead beetle in my tea the month before. I'd shrugged it off—bugs are everywhere in Florida—and requested a fresh pot of tea. Ever since then, we'd been treated like special guests by the owner, probably because we didn't make a fuss or report him to the county health inspector.

Beetle tea aside, it was a nice little restaurant. The owner's mother, who had apparently been dead for years, always stood near the kitchen door and kept an eye on the dining room. I was the only one in the restaurant who knew she was there; I never spoke to her, but she always smiled and nodded when she saw me. She threw a fit on

Beetle Night, screeching at her son in heated Mandarin while he simultaneously apologized to us. Mama Chen didn't appreciate customers being served buggy tea in her restaurant.

After an insect-free meal at Mama Chen's, Dad insisted on buying me five more white polos. Only then was he satisfied that I wouldn't have to go to school shirtless.

On the way home, I stared out the window. Palmetto Crossing was small and pretty, in a boring manicured-lawns-and-backyard-swimming-pools kind of way, and it was full of palm trees and old people, just like the rest of Florida. You couldn't throw a rock anywhere in the state without hitting a retiree or a coconut palm. Lakewood had been a lot like that, too, but I had a reluctant preference for Palmetto Crossing because Aunt Thelma didn't live there.

Dad unlocked the door to the front parlor and reset the security alarm. We were halfway up the stairs to the apartment when we heard the thumping. Dad froze and motioned for me to stay back, but I already knew where the noise was coming from.

"Crap. Buster!" I pushed past Dad into the apartment, where the trunk was rocking irately in the little living room.

Dad followed me in and looked down at the trunk in dismay. "You didn't let him out before we left?"

"I forgot. He's going to be mad."

"For once, I can't blame him."

"Stand back; this won't be pretty." I pulled the curved obsidian free and opened the trunk. An icy blast hit me in the face with enough force to send me stumbling backward against Dad. Buster scolded me with an insulted moan, and books began hurtling through the living room and banging against the walls.

Ugh. Not again.

It took about fifteen minutes and three cookies (oatmeal chocolate chip—Buster's favorite—I tossed them into the air and they disappeared) to get him to settle down, and another half hour to clean up his mess. While Dad and I gathered books by the armful, I kept an eye out for *Wuthering Heights*. When I found it, I flipped it open while Dad wasn't looking and made sure the Palmetto Paranormal business card was still inside. It was. I kept meaning to put it somewhere safer, but at the same time, I kind of felt like I was honoring Mom's memory by leaving it exactly where she had.

When we were done, Dad pointed to his watch. "It's getting late. You have to be at the bus stop at six forty-five, so maybe you should think about going to bed."

"Bleh." I ignored his suggestion and flopped down on the couch. I was still thinking about the business card. "Tell me something about Mom. What was it like doing those investigations with her?"

He looked over from where he was straightening a pile of books. "Where'd that come from?"

"I don't know." I almost felt brave enough to mention my plan to follow in her footsteps. Almost. "I've just been thinking about her lately. Tell me something I don't know."

"You remember your mother just fine."

"Yeah, but there's plenty I don't know, right? Tell me about one of the investigations you guys did."

I knew he wouldn't. And he definitely wouldn't tell me what I most needed to hear: what really happened during the investigation of the Logan Street house on Riley Island the night Mom died.

Occasionally I thought about finding a way to figure it out by myself.

Okay, I thought about it every single day.

"Well . . ." He looked relieved when his cell phone rang. He unclipped it from his belt and answered, then listened and said, "I'm so sorry. I'll be right there," and hung up. "Sorry, kiddo. Ralph Wilson's mother just passed away at home. I need to get over there and help take care of things. Should take a few hours. You'll be okay by yourself, right?"

I nodded. Nighttime calls like that were common; some people were pretty inconsiderate about what time of day they decided to die, so independent funeral directors and morticians like my dad didn't have the luxury of regular business hours. Dad kept throwing around the idea of hiring an assistant, but he didn't have the budget for it yet, so he carried the full responsibility of the business on his shoulders. (Well, except for that unpaid, underage, massively talented intern he had handling the death spackle and babysitting the poltergeist.)

He kissed my forehead on his way out. "I might not see you before you leave tomorrow morning, so have a great first day at school."

"I'm sure it'll be amazing and fantastic and splendiferous," I said drily as he left.

That phone call might have saved him, but Dad's reluctance to talk about Mom was nothing new. He still missed her, and he dealt with his grief by not dwelling on her memory. But I missed her, too, and I didn't have as many memories of her as he did, and that wasn't fair.

There was another reason talking about Mom made Dad uncomfortable. He never came right out and said it, but I could tell it was always there, this dread right below the surface. He was afraid I might have seen her and maybe talked to her at some point after she died, and he couldn't handle the thought of his wife as a ghost. A ghost he couldn't see the way I could.

Not that there was any reason for him to worry. No matter how many times I wished, and how hard I tried to sense her presence, Mom never appeared to me. She wasn't around. I knew I shouldn't take it personally, but I did. I'd hoped that moving back in with Dad would alleviate that feeling somehow, as though being close to him again would also let me feel closer to her. It didn't, though, and I was starting to realize that if I really wanted to get past the doubts I still had about the night Mom died, I'd have to find the truth myself.

But first I had a far more pressing horror to deal with: Palmetto High.

CHAPTER two
wipe your feet

Monday morning arrived much too quickly. The idea of breakfast or even coffee made my stomach flip in all kinds of unpleasant ways, so I forced down a glass of milk, then got dressed. White collared shirt, khaki pants—ugh. I know being miserable is basically part of my job as a high school student, but Palmetto was making it way too easy. I missed the dark-wash jeans and purple or black shirts I'd been allowed to wear at Lakewood, which didn't have a dress code.

Palmetto High's "rules of fashion" didn't say much about jewelry, aside from a prohibition on piercings anywhere except the earlobes, so at least I could still wear my dangly purple spider earrings. I'd bought them last year from Striped Skull at the mall, mostly to annoy Aunt Thelma, who always tried to steer me in the direction of little gold hoops or pearl studs. I didn't bother with makeup, except for a little lip gloss. I laced up my purple high-top Chuck Taylors, and glopped a coat of quick-dry purple polish on my fingernails. I always make sure to have on some purple somewhere—it's my favorite color, and it had been Mom's favorite as well.

I'd heard Dad get home well after midnight, and he was in the shower when I was getting ready for school. I had already registered at Palmetto, but he'd offered to drive me on the first day and help me get everything sorted out at the front office. I'd said I didn't need him to do that. If spending time with Aunt Thelma had given me anything, it was an independent streak. She was the kind of person who'd expect a kindergartner to find his own classroom on the first day of school. She certainly hadn't walked me inside on my first day as a freshman at Lakewood last year, and I didn't need anyone to hold my hand at Palmetto, either.

Before leaving the apartment, I checked the contents of my messenger bag. I'd thrown in a couple of notebooks and pens and pencils, my cell phone and MP3 player, and the black zippered pouch I use as a wallet. The last thing in the bag was a little leather bag of gemstones and crystals. They'd belonged to Mom. She'd thought they were lucky and protective, especially her favorite: a tumbled pebble of shiny black tourmaline. I wasn't so sure about the luck thing, but I liked having them with me.

Aunt Thelma had lived a block from Lakewood High, so I'd been able to walk to school last year. Attending Palmetto meant riding the bus instead. After ten minutes of wilting in the stifling morning humidity at the bus stop and another twenty sitting in an unair-conditioned, slightly ripe bus, my bangs were sticking to my face and I could feel sweat trickling down between my shoulder blades. I was dragging, and I regretted skipping my coffee that morning. At that moment I would've just about traded five years of my life for an iced latte.

After filing off the bus with the rest of the herd, I stared in dismay at the collection of buildings in front of me. Palmetto looked even bigger now than it had last week. Its district covered Palmetto Crossing plus some of the smaller towns nearby, and its student body was nearly four times larger than Lakewood's. Surrounded by palm trees and spindly Australian pines that flagged slightly in the hot breeze, the campus consisted of four two-story buildings connected by covered walkways. The buildings were arranged around a big central courtyard with a few scraggly planters and a huge sundial in the middle that looked like the ideal spot for Aztec-style blood sacrifices. A row of portable classrooms sat around back.

The bus loop was off to one side, near the senior parking lot; from there I managed to fight my way to the main office. What a freakin' zoo. I'd probably gone to elementary school with at least some of the herd plodding around me, but I hadn't kept in touch with anyone after I'd left the Palmetto school district.

When I'd registered the week before, the sophomore guidance counselor explained that returning students had signed up for this semester's electives last spring, so some classes were already full. She wrote down my preferences— Intro to Drawing and Intro to Film I, along with Pottery I and Intro to Poetry as alternates. Intro to Poetry sounded pretty dreadful, but it was still better than the other choices, most of which were gym-related. Gym and I seriously don't get along.

So, of course, when the secretary at the front desk looked me up in the system and printed my schedule, the first class listed was Beginning Gym.

"No way," I said. "This is a mistake."

The secretary glared at me over the rim of her glasses; I guess my complaint wasn't the first one she'd heard that morning. "Any problems must be handled by your guidance counselor. There's a sign-up sheet over there on the counter. Write down your name, and she'll see you as soon as possible."

"But—"

"There's nothing I can do. Write down your name and go to class."

"Fine." Judging by the eight million names already on

the sign-up sheet, the entire sophomore class was just as delighted with their schedules as I was. It would take the whole semester for the counselor to go through them all.

There was no pen on the counter, so I fished my own out of my messenger bag. I was about to write my name at the bottom of the sheet when I noticed a name in pencil, just a few lines down from the top: Emerson Bean. What kind of name was that? It sounded like it belonged to an uptight, snooty old man who signed his name with "Esq." and spent the evenings in his study, smoking a pipe, alone.

After glancing at the secretary and making sure she was busy berating another unhappy student, I found a pencil in my bag, erased good ol' Emerson, and wrote my name in his place—in ink. *Sorry, Emerson, old chap,* I thought. *But, you know . . . Freakin' gym! This is an emergency.*

I loitered for a moment longer, until the secretary looked up and made a shooing motion—like I was a pesky mosquito buzzing in her ear. "Go to class," she repeated. "You'll be called down for an appointment as soon as possible."

Meh. *Gym.* I considered hiding in the library or the nearest bathroom until first period was over, but skipping class usually meant detention, and detention meant spending even more time at school. I could stomach gym for one day. After all, it was the first day of class, and nothing ever happened on the first day.

Feeling like a clueless freshman, I checked the map in the school handbook and crossed the courtyard in the general direction of the gym. On the way, I looked over the rest of my schedule. At least there were no other disasters listed. I'd even gotten a fifth-period drawing class as my other elective.

I crossed onto one of the walkways and stepped into another building, where I ended up at one end of a long hallway. One side of the hall was lined with trophy cases. The other sported the most god-awful mural I'd ever seen—a crooked, disproportionate, yellow-and-green Trojan warrior with a football impaled on his sword. Wow. Had the principal lost a bet with another school or something?

A set of double doors, one green and one yellow, loomed ominously at the end of the hallway. Heading toward them was like making that final stroll to the execution chamber. Dead girl walking.

Maybe it sounds overdramatic, but I don't think it's possible to express how much I hate gym.

Hoping the guidance counselor was zipping down the line of discontented sophomores at somewhere near the speed of sound, I pushed open the gym doors and slipped inside.

Immediately, a basketball came flying at my face. I screamed and ducked; the ball bounced off the top of my head, which hurt, but not as much as if it had smacked me on the nose.

"Hey!" A beer-gutted man in a green-and-yellow cap stalked over, a whistle on a lanyard bouncing against his wide chest. "You're supposed to come in through the locker room entrance."

I rubbed my throbbing scalp.

"Sorry, I didn't know. I'm looking for . . ." I paused and glanced at my schedule. "Beginning Gym with Coach . . . Frucile. Is that you?"

"No, I'm Coach Perelli," the man snarled, as though I'd committed an unforgivable sin just by approaching him. "Coach Frucile's back there." He jammed a thumb over his shoulder toward a group gathered at the other end of the gym. When he turned back to the tall boys, his stomach jiggled under his Palmetto High Basketball T-shirt.

I made my way around the perimeter of the gym, keeping an eye out in case any more rogue sports equipment decided to attack. The pain in my head was down to a minor pounding, but I wondered if I should tell this Frucile person what had happened. Maybe I'd get sent to the school nurse. Regardless of whether I was actually hurt, sitting in the nurse's office sounded a lot better—and safer—than staying here.

Before I could speak up, though, a muscular woman

with short red hair beat me to it. "Beginning Gym? You're late! Name!" she barked.

It took me a second to realize she'd meant that as a question. "Um, Violet Addison."

"Addison." She held a clipboard with what I assumed was an attendance sheet, but she seemed to freeze for a moment when she heard my name. She looked up, focused on me, blinked. "You're Addison."

"Um, yeah."

She paused for another second, then made a mark on the clipboard. Weird.

I tried for sympathy. "I just got hit with a basketball, and—"

"Basketball unit isn't until November. Get in line." Behind her, the class stood in four straight, timid lines.

"Okay, but—"

"You've already missed five minutes of orientation. In line!"

Her tone made me panicky. "Which line?"

"Pick one!"

If I'd had a tail, I would've tucked it between my legs. I left my bag near the wall with the others and retreated meekly to the shortest line. My face felt hot; being singled out always makes me blush, something that's mortifyingly obvious when you're as pale as I am. The coach went back to her orientation speech, yammering about attendance and doctor's notes and gym clothes. Since I had no intention of staying in her class, I tuned out until I heard her holler, "Addison!"

Oh, what now?

"Get up here. I'm using you as an example of inappropriate footwear."

The lead weight in the pit of my stomach turned into a total cannonball. I trudged up beside her, while everyone stared at me.

She pointed to my feet, but she addressed the entire group. "I don't want to see shoes like this in my class. Proper sneakers only."

I looked down at my poor, defenseless Chucks. "These are sneakers."

"No arch support, bad traction, poorly padded soles," she rattled off. "Make sure you have acceptable athletic shoes when we start dressing out next week. And those of you with long hair like this," she continued, still gesturing toward me, "make sure it's pulled back. Addison, back in line."

Fuming, I obeyed her latest command, letting my hair fall in my face in defiance.

Ten minutes later she called over Coach Perelli, and they both walked us to the locker rooms. There the group split into girls and boys. Perelli followed the boys into their locker room, while Frucile followed the girls into ours.

Everything was okay for about three seconds. Then I felt it. I felt it and I wanted to run. Something supernatural was in the locker room with us, and it wasn't anything I wanted to know better. It built up around me like a storm cloud, all anger and rage, and hot, clammy fear, and the longer I stood there, the stronger it grew. It came from everywhere at once in the too-warm room. I felt its clammy tendrils wrapping around me, pulling me deeper, closer, toward a darkened alcove to the right.

It usually takes a lot to scare me, but five minutes in the girls' locker room did the trick.

The presence was so strong—why couldn't anyone else feel it? My classmates stood around looking bored and fiddling with their lockers while Frucile continued her orientation lecture, barking louder and faster than ever.

"School-approved locks only! Locks are five dollars, which you'll get back at the end of the semester if you return the lock in working condition. My office is over there," she said, pointing to a closed-off space to the left of the main changing area. "And the showers are right here." She walked to the dark alcove and hit a wall switch. A row of fluorescent ceiling lights buzzed to life, revealing a series of tiled stalls sporting meager green-and-yellow shower curtains.

There was something so wrong in that alcove. You

could've covered me in mud and dog crap, and I still wouldn't have showered in there. I guess Frucile kept talking; I couldn't hear her over the blood drumming in my ears. As the thing and its endless, invisible dread swirled around me—trapping, constricting—the edges of my vision began to go white. The air around me went freezing cold, then swelteringly hot again. I couldn't breathe.

I needed to get out of there. I spun around and went back into the gym. If the coach called after me, I didn't hear. I couldn't. There was only the roar of my pulse and that thing's silent yet deafening rage.

Back in the gym, I bent over, resting my hands on my knees. I could finally fill my lungs again; I had never before appreciated the simple luxury of a deep breath. I had no idea what had just happened; all I knew was that I'd never encountered anything like that before, and I was never, ever going back in that locker room. Whatever was in there, it couldn't have been a ghost. Mom had taught me when I was little that ghosts might be scary, but they were never threatening or just plain evil. That thing in there, though? Totally evil. The lead cannonball in my stomach grew roots and became an anchor.

I was still catching my breath when the class filed back in, chased by Coach Frucile.

"Addison!" she said when she saw me. "I don't

appreciate you leaving in the middle of orientation."

"Asthma attack," I lied. "My inhaler was in my bag." I hoped she wouldn't ask to see the inhaler as proof, since I didn't have one.

"Don't think you'll be able to use that as an excuse in my class without a doctor's note," she said. Then she clapped her hands and went back to yelling at everyone instead of just me. "Get back in your lines. These are your teams for the semester. We have just enough time for a volleyball intro before the bell rings."

The anchor grew big enough to ground a cruise ship.

"Addison! You serve." Coach Frucile lobbed a volleyball at me. I screamed and jumped aside to avoid another collision; my left sneaker skidded on the freshly varnished floor, and I fell backward onto my butt.

"That's why I require proper sneakers," Coach Frucile told the class.

Screw this. It wasn't like I was staying in the class, so I didn't need to play nice with Coach Frucile, especially since she was so hell-bent on picking on me. Embarrassed tears pricked my eyes as I grabbed my bag and left— through the side entrance this time. I ducked into a nearby restroom and waited until the bell rang; it took me that long to stop shaking.

I had Algebra II second period, but I was only in class

for ten minutes before a student aide from the guidance office showed up with a slip of paper bearing my name. Sweet. Meanwhile, poor Emerson Bean, Esq., sat in a classroom somewhere, miserably waiting to be summoned.

I was ushered into the office of Mrs. Ortiz, the sophomore guidance counselor. Mrs. Ortiz already had my transcript and schedule pulled up on her computer; she smiled pleasantly but blankly across her desk, giving no sign that she remembered me from when I'd registered the week before. She had tired eyes with dark bags underneath.

"Hi, Violet. What seems to be the trouble?"

"I'm in the wrong class," I said, sitting down.

Her eyes darted back and forth as she skimmed my schedule on her monitor. "I'm not seeing a problem. Which class?"

"Beginning Gym." I shivered, still shaken from my freaky locker-room experience. "I was supposed to have Intro to Film."

"Hmm." She hit a few keys. "Nope. Intro to Film is full. We had to place you elsewhere."

"I picked alternates, too. Intro to Poetry. Pottery."

"I'm afraid those are full as well."

I tried to remember the other choices. "I'll take anything that isn't gym. Home Ec? Chorus? Drama? Intro to Basket Weaving?"

Mrs. Ortiz chuckled but shook her head. "I don't see any alternatives that'll fit your schedule. Stick with gym for now. It's a requirement for graduation anyway, so you might as well get it out of the way."

Ohhhh, no. No way. "I took a semester of gym last year at Lakewood; I already have that credit."

She looked at my records again. "I don't . . . Oh, okay. Personal Fitness. A Personal Fitness credit from the Brevard County school system can't be transferred as a gym credit here. They're categorized differently."

"But it was a gym class! With awful gym clothes and grumpy coaches and basketballs hitting me in the head, just like here!"

"I understand that, but the system won't let me reclassify the credit on your transcript."

"So I'm stuck?"

"It's just a semester, Violet."

Yeah, a semester of drowning in horror in that locker room.

"Coach Frucile and I don't get along. I already left today's class early because she threw a volleyball at me."

"I'll write you a note and say you were meeting with me." Mrs. Ortiz scribbled on a pad and tore off the top sheet. "Give her that tomorrow. She'll excuse you for today."

Out of arguments, I took the note and left. Maybe

Dad would be okay with me serving daily detentions for the rest of the semester. That was exactly what I'd be doing, since I intended to skip first period every day until the spring.

Returning to Algebra II meant crossing from one building to another. There was a puddle in the walkway, probably from one of Florida's regular afternoon showers the day before. I splashed through it without a thought, went inside, and squelched down the hallway toward my classroom.

"Do you mind?" someone said behind me. The voice was gruff and familiar. "I just mopped that!"

I yelped a little in surprise and spun around. "Henry?"

Sure enough, the ghostly janitor stood a few feet away, busily mopping. "Yeah, who else? Told you I worked for the school system, didn't I?"

"Sorry, I was just—"

"Look at that mess." He jabbed his mop at my wet footprints. "And this darn thing ain't good for nothing anymore." Apparently the giddiness he'd felt at the thought of going back to his job instead of finding his wife had worn off.

"I didn't mean to—"

"Darn kids today don't have any respect. Didn't your mother ever teach you to wipe your feet?"

And that was when my patience—what was left of it—gave out. "Oh, shut up, newbie," I said, forgetting to keep my voice low. "Either cross over or quit your bitching!"

"Violet?"

I glanced over to where Mrs. Brown, my Algebra II teacher, stared curiously at me from the classroom doorway. Oh crap.

"Everything okay?" she asked uncertainly.

"Um, yeah." I shrugged.

"Why don't you come back in, then?" She spoke in the sort of soothing tone one might use on a seriously unstable person, and since she'd just seen me apparently talking to myself, she probably thought that was the case.

I nodded and returned to my seat, ignoring the stares I got along the way. Everyone in the class had apparently heard my little outburst; I hadn't done my reputation any favors with that one.

CHAPTER THREE
Ghost Jock and ~~Gabriel Saint Rochester~~
Rochester Saint Gabriel

The state of Florida has this funny habit of building or renovating schools so that they're just big enough for the current population of the district, which means they start running out of room as soon as more families move nearby. Palmetto High is more than sixty years old; it's the oldest school in the area, and its last renovation was more than five years ago, which explained the bank of portables out back. Connected by a crooked, hastily poured concrete walkway, the trailers sat in a marshy field, the kind of not-quite-swampland that floods and attracts snakes during the rainy season, and wasps all year long.

Palmetto's overcrowding also explained the chronic lack of seating in the cafeteria. After fourth period I walked into the packed room, surveyed the clique-segregated tables—populars, jocks, emos, goths, punks, and every other kid who was happy to fit into a pre-established mold—and walked back out. Definitely not my kind of thing. Since I couldn't wander the school without a hall pass, I ducked into a stairwell and waited for the bell.

After my bizarre morning, it was with great relief that I finally headed to the art wing for Intro to Drawing. On the way, a loud crash in the hall made me glance over my shoulder. A couple of bigger guys in Palmetto football jerseys had shoved this short, skinny kid into the locker bank as they went by. Jerks. It's not so bad being ignored when that's the alternative.

Palmetto's drawing room was big and airy; it was a corner room, with huge windows on two walls letting in lots of natural light. The industrial tile floor was splattered with years of spilled paint, the brightness of which made me think of a new box of crayons.

Mr. Connelly, the drawing teacher, stood by the door, checking off names and giving instructions. "We've got two classes in here this period," he said. "If you're here for Intro to Drawing, tape a piece of newsprint to one of those drawing boards and pick a bench on the right side of the room." Most of the students in the room had moved to the right; it looked like only two were in the more advanced class on the left. They were left alone to do as they pleased for the most part. Luckies.

Like most intro-level electives, Intro to Drawing had everything from overeager freshmen to uninterested seniors who just needed an art credit to graduate. Once my class was settled, Mr. Connelly gave the usual orientation spiel. Then he explained that we'd be studying perspective first, and he told us to sketch a view of the classroom from our seats, paying special attention to angles and lines.

I'd barely penciled in the walls and floor when someone behind me hissed, "Hey!" Figuring the hisser was talking to a friend, I ignored him.

He didn't give up, though.

"Hey, girl with the black hair!"

I wasn't in the mood. Continuing to ignore him, I sketched in the windows.

Then something brushed by my feet. I looked down to see my messenger bag sliding slowly away from me. I stomped on one corner, pinning it in place, then turned to glare at the sandy-haired guy tugging on the strap.

"Quit it."

It was one of the bullies from the hallway, the ones wearing the Palmetto jerseys. I hoped he'd gotten detention for not following the dress code. He grinned at me with the kind of perfect teeth that were probably sporting a full set of braces a year or two earlier—with green and yellow spacers, I bet. More interestingly, a ghost was peering curiously over his shoulder. The ghost also wore a jersey. Dress codes don't mean much when you're dead.

"How come you didn't answer me?" the guy asked.

"I'm busy."

"You're that Addison chick, right?"

"Why?"

"Your dad runs that funeral home."

The guy turned to his fellow jersey-wearing jocks. "See? Told you it was her."

A blond girl squinted at me. "And you seriously live right there in the funeral home? How can you stand it with all those dead bodies around?" She wore a snug yellow T-shirt with CHEERLEADER and a palmetto leaf printed in green across the chest. How come no one seemed to be following the dress code but me?

"It's just my dad's job. And we live upstairs. Not with the bodies."

Cheerleader wrinkled her nose. "Doesn't it smell?"

Oh, I *so* did not have the patience for this garbage. "The bodies are nothing. It's the ghosts you gotta watch out for." I gave Ghost Jock a pointed I-see-you glance, then stood up and moved to another bench.

Some ghosts know right away that I can see them; it takes others longer to catch on, and Ghost Jock was apparently of the slower variety. His eyes widened and followed me. Like Henry the janitor, he was blue and filmy and translucent.

"Is she serious?" Cheerleader whispered to the head jock.

"Don't be a dumbass, Cherry," Head Jock said back.

(*Cherry? Really? Come on.* Her name matched her glittery red lip gloss, and that was just sad.)

"But I heard she freaked out in the hall this morning."

"She's making it up."

I went back and stood beside Head Jock and quietly said, "I think the ghost standing behind you would back me up." I knew I was committing some kind of popularity suicide by squaring off against a jock and a cheerleader this early in the year, but I didn't care. I hated them on principle.

Ghost Jock rolled his eyes and gestured for me to be quiet.

"What the hell do you mean?" Head Jock glanced around.

"He's tall, dark haired, and he's wearing a Palmetto jersey. Number Forty-eight. Friend of yours?" I grabbed a fresh sheet of newsprint and went to a different drawing bench.

Mr. Connelly had been helping another student figure out the angles of the ceiling, but he glanced up when he saw I was moving around. "Is there a problem?"

"Nope. Just wanted another perspective," I said.

He nodded. "Next time, though, pick a spot and stick with it. All right?"

I nodded and got settled again, then started sketching furiously, trying to finish. I was angry and elated and terrified at the same time. Why had I done that? I'd just outed myself and the whole ghost thing to the entire class.

I could still hear Head Jock and Cherry Cheerleader muttering to each other. Cherry looked almost agitated enough to cry—not a good idea, considering the gobs of mascara she wore. "How could she know about Dirk?"

"Lucky guess?" Head Jock was shaken, too, although he was making a huge effort to hide it.

"The accident was two years ago!"

"It was big news. She probably saw it on TV or something. Or maybe she memorizes obituaries when she's not busy hanging out with dead bodies."

Cherry shook her head. "I don't know. That was really spooky."

Still standing nearby, Ghost Jock, otherwise known as Dead Dirk, glared at me and gave me the finger. Now that was interesting. The ghosts who didn't want me around were most often the ones with unfinished business. They were unsettled and fussy, not ready to accept the reality of their deaths. I figured Dead Dirk was still hanging around his teammates because he just wasn't ready to man up and move on.

I got maybe five more minutes of sketching done before someone tapped me on the shoulder. "Busy," I muttered.

"Can you really see ghosts and stuff?" It was a boy's voice again, but hesitant and genuine and almost hopeful instead of teasing and disdainful.

I sighed, leaned my drawing board against the front of the bench, and turned to my right. "Yeah. Why?"

It was the boy I'd seen get pushed into the lockers. He was small, with the kind of slightly awkward features he might eventually grow into. His black hair, an obvious home dye job, was tousled and unkempt, and he had dark eyeliner smudged around his eyes. Unlike the jocks and Cherry, he wore the requisite collared shirt and khaki trousers, but he'd doodled in permanent ink on the left knee of his pants, and despite the late August heat, he wore black-and-white striped arm warmers that ended in fingerless gloves. *Cheer up, emo kid,* I thought.

"You're Violet, right?" he asked.

I narrowed my eyes a little. "Yeah. And?"

"The same Violet who went to Palmetto Elementary?"

Well, this was a different line of questioning. I nodded; that was where I'd gone to school before switching districts.

"We were both in Mrs. Green's class in second grade."

"Oh. Okay." No lightbulbs of recognition went off.

"I'm Tim Williams. We sat at the same table when

Mrs. Green made us do those science activities in groups."

I vaguely recalled something about sitting in groups of four while Mrs. Green frumped around the room and made us do boring experiments with things like magnets. Magnets! Oh yeah. "You're the kid who swallowed a magnet that one day."

Any thrill over being remembered was flushed right out of him. "I went to the emergency room because of that."

It was all coming back to me. Timmy Williams had had light brown hair and huge teeth. He'd worn T-shirts with puppies on them, and he'd had a habit of picking his nose and eating whatever he dug out. He looked pretty different now. I hoped his eating habits had also changed.

"So anyway," he said, "that's cool about the ghosts."

"Uh, okay." No one had ever described my abilities as "cool" before.

"What's it like? Do you get to cross them over and send them into the light and all that stuff?"

I tried to draw and whisper at the same time. "Not really. I mostly just see them around. I can talk to them, but they don't always feel like talking back."

Tim looked almost enthralled. "Is Dirk Reynolds really here?"

"Number Forty-eight? Yeah, he's over there with the other jocks. What happened to him?"

"Car accident a couple of years ago. He was a junior when those guys up there were all freshmen; they're juniors now. Do you really live in a funeral home?"

I sighed. "Above, not in. My dad owns Addison Funeral Services, and we live in the apartment upstairs."

"Sweet. Maybe I can come over some time."

"Seriously, Timmy?" I tried to pay attention to my sketch.

"It's Tim. Not Timmy. But I'm changing it as soon as I turn eighteen, anyway. I'm going to be Gabriel Saint Rochester."

I paused, the point of my pencil pressed against the paper. "There's no Saint Rochester."

"I know, but it sounds so cool."

"So why not use Rochester Saint Gabriel instead? At least there *was* a Saint Gabriel."

"Rochester Saint Gabriel . . ." He mulled it over. "Awesome. I can use that?"

"Knock yourself out. But why do you want to be a Rochester instead of a Tim?"

"It matches my nature," he said somberly. I could tell he wanted me to ask what he meant by that, but I didn't feel like it. "You should hang out with us soon."

"'Us?'"

"Me and my friends. They'd like you."

"Why?"

"Well . . . we're into the whole goth thing, too."

"I thought you were emo."

He looked a little put out.

I shrugged. "Sorry. But no, I'm not goth." I kind of hate it when people make assumptions like that. Just because I have black hair and pale skin and wear a lot of black and think about death a lot . . . Okay, I see where they get it. I'm not goth, though. I'm not emo, I'm not punk, I'm not scene, I'm not any of that. I'm just me, and I don't like being stereotyped.

"Oh. Well, my friends would like you anyway. And Isobel's been kind of wanting to meet you, so if you'd let me introduce you, I could, you know, score some points . . ." His voice trailed off and he looked sort of embarrassed.

I felt bad for the kid. Clearly he needed help upping his cool factor, and being pushed around by the jocks wasn't doing him any favors. Plus, he did think seeing ghosts was cool. . . .

"Fine," I said. "Take me to your goths, Rochester Saint Gabriel."

It turned out Tim and I also had the same Chemistry class sixth period, so we walked there together. On the way, near a bank of lockers, Tim spotted a group of somber-looking kids and dragged me over. Several of them nodded at him, but one tall girl—the only one who'd ignored the dress code and looked legitimately spooky—ignored him.

Of course, she was the one he chose to address, which told me who she was even before he said her name. "Hi, Isobel," he said, slightly hesitant.

Instead of returning the greeting, she rolled her eyes and pursed her dark red lips. "What?"

Tim took a step back as if he thought she might bite. She certainly looked capable of it—her pale skin and elaborate, dark eye makeup made her look almost vampiric, and she wore a corseted black dress that looked straight out of *Dracula*. She had long black hair and short bangs that were shot through with streaks of red, and her overly arched eyebrows might have left her looking constantly surprised if the rest of her expression weren't so sour.

"This, uh," Tim stammered, "this is . . ."

"I'm Violet Addison," I said, to save his skin. It might've taken him all of sixth period to finish his sentence.

Isobel's eyes widened, and now she really did look surprised. "You're the funeral home girl?"

"That would be me."

"She talks to ghosts, too." Tim threw in helpfully.

Isobel looked extremely interested in this, but the warning bell rang, saving me from further explanation.

"Gotta go!" I said, grabbing Tim's sleeve and pulling him away. "See you around!"

We made our way to chem, and I could tell Tim was sulking.

"She wanted to talk to us!" He pouted. "Don't you realize how rare it is for a junior like Isobel to even acknowledge me?"

"And now she'll want to talk to us again," I said. "Always leave 'em wanting more." Not that I was at all interested in another goth encounter, but Tim obviously had a thing for Isobel, and I felt kind of oddly protective. In some ways, he seemed as weird as me, and that made me want to help him out. Kind of.

"So what's with the dress code?" I asked, choosing a lab table and stowing my bag under my stool. "Isobel sure wasn't following it."

"Her, in a white polo? She'd have to be dead first."

"She kind of looked that way already."

Tim grinned a little. "The dress code's not really in effect the first week of school. She'll look like that all year, though. She'll get a week of suspension, but she doesn't care."

"What about the jocks in drawing?"

He snorted dismissively. "Them? Like they have to follow any of the rules."

"They don't have to wear these stupid uniforms?"

"Not as long as they're wearing something related to Palmetto sports."

That sucked. "So just because they can catch a ball or knock people down or do backflips—"

"What, you thought high school was for learning?"

We both snickered at that. Nothing cements a friendship as quickly as shared disdain.

CHAPTER FOUR
no respect for half vampires

After the last bell, Tim followed me to the bus loop like a lost puppy and asked if he could please, please visit Addison Funeral Services. At first I wished he'd go away; I really didn't feel like being shadowed anymore and I had a lot on my mind with the whole locker-room thing. Then a couple of jocks in Palmetto jerseys walked by on their way to the student parking lot. One of them—I recognized him from drawing class—saw Tim and paused like he'd just spotted easy prey. I realized Tim was probably in for more harassment if I left him on his own, so I agreed to his request and quickly led him away from the jocks and toward my bus. He could be annoying, but that didn't mean I wanted him to get his butt kicked. I gave the jock the stink eye over my shoulder as we retreated.

Dad was still working on Ralph Wilson's mother when we got to the mortuary. Luckily, she didn't seem to be around to cause any trouble. I introduced Tim, so he at least got a peek at the embalming room. Then I showed him around the rest of the downstairs and explained the ins and outs of death spackle. He was fascinated; I wondered if that was genuine, or if he was just trying to be a good goth.

When we went upstairs, I tried to open the door to the apartment, but it wouldn't budge. It wasn't locked; the knob turned easily. I gave it a short shove and managed to open it a few inches, but then it slammed in my face like someone was blocking it from the other side.

"You know, I should probably tell you about Buster before we go in," I said, pushing against the door with my shoulder but not really expecting it to give. I'd silently debated whether to introduce Tim to Buster. I suppose I could have gone up by myself and put Buster in his crate before letting Tim into the apartment, but Tim was so enthusiastic I couldn't resist letting him have the full abnormal-poltergeist experience. Plus, I kind of wanted to mess with him. "Buster's sort of—*OOF!*" The door opened easily this time, and I went sprawling into the living room, which was freezing. My breath came out in visible puffs.

Behind me, Tim stepped into the room and stared. The door slammed shut behind him, and what little color there'd been in his face drained away. The living room was upside down. All the furniture—the corduroy couch and two chairs, the coffee table, the TV cabinet, even the filled bookcases—hung down from the ceiling as if they'd been anchored in place. The room echoed with happy, mischievous screams.

I stood up. "This is pretty typical. He's showing off. Don't react; you'll just encourage him."

But Tim was already backing away. He pressed against the door; when he couldn't open it, he crossed the room in a panic, gawking up at the furniture overhead instead of looking where he was going. He was headed toward the living room window, and although I didn't think he could actually go through it, he was moving fast enough to hurt himself if he kept going.

"Look out!" I said. Before I could reach out and yank him back, the couch flipped down from the ceiling and thudded to the floor in front of him, so that Tim tripped and toppled on to it. While he righted himself, the rest of the furniture drifted back into place.

Tim was trembling violently; he looked like he might throw up.

"What was that?"

"That was Buster."

"When you said you had to tell me about him, I thought you were talking about a dog."

"That's not so far from the truth," I said as Buster's

favorite toy—a squeaky vinyl hamburger—sailed through the air toward Tim. I grabbed it before it could smack into him and tossed it down the hall.

"Go get it, Buster!" The burger's squeaks soon mingled with Buster's happy cries.

Tim calmed down after I ushered him into the kitchen. I thought about offering him soda, but he didn't look like he needed any caffeine, and he looked grateful when I suggested chamomile tea instead. Buster tried to follow us; when I told him to bug off, he acknowledged my command by grabbing my hair and twisting it into a knot. After being threatened with the crate, though, he went back to his squeaky burger.

Tim stared warily at the kitchen doorway, as though he'd be able to see if Buster came back again.

"It's okay," I said, putting the water on to boil. "You can tell he's nearby when the temperature in the room drops, but he'd never actually hurt anyone. At least, not intentionally. He just likes to play jokes."

"What is he?"

"We don't really know. I call him an abnormal poltergeist." I explained how Buster had come to live with us. "I'm not used to having guests, and I'm so used to him that I forget he might startle other people."

Tim raised a brow, indicating that *startle* was too weak a word.

I suddenly felt a little defensive about Buster, the same way a bulldog owner might feel if someone said his dog's wrinkled face was ugly.

"Come on, he's okay. Besides, I thought you said the whole ghost thing was cool."

"That was before I actually met one," Tim said, but he seemed to be unwinding a little.

"Ghosts aren't all like Buster," I said after pouring the tea. "Most of them don't cause trouble like he does unless they're agitated." Like that awful presence in the locker room. "They're usually harmless; they just stick around to keep an eye on things." I told him about Mama Chen. "You'd never even know she was there."

Retaining a little of his earlier curiosity, Tim said, "We should go to Mama Chen's sometime. Maybe I'll be able to see her like you can."

"If you could see ghosts, you'd know."

"What about Buster? Can you see him?"

"No, but he's not a good example. He's just weird. There's no one set of rules they all follow. And not all ghosts are visible, either, so sometimes I can sense ghosts, but I can't see them. I can see most of them, though."

"How'd you first find out you could see them?"

"I've seen them for as long as I can remember. But it took me a long time to understand that not everyone could see what I could, and that ghosts weren't the same as living people." I told him about the time Dad and I were on our way to pick up Mom at the airport; she'd flown out to Texas for a few days to help a cousin with some possible paranormal activity in a new apartment. A big accident had backed up traffic on the highway, and we inched past the remains of a crushed SUV and an overturned school bus. It must have been pretty grisly, because Dad told me not to look. But I wasn't looking at the wreckage; I was more interested in all the confused blue kids who were wandering around, darting past the slow-moving traffic and sometimes passing right through cars. I remember saying something to Dad about how kids shouldn't walk in the middle of the highway. Of course, he couldn't see what I was referring to. I was only three years old, but that was when Dad could no longer deny that I had the same abilities as my mom.

Mom, of course, had realized this much earlier— when I was just a few months old. When I was six, she told me about the day she took me for a walk in my stroller past old Mr. Albertson's house. Mr. Albertson had died years earlier, but he'd built that house with his own hands, and he wasn't about to leave. As long as its new owners took good care of the place, he was a very polite, quiet ghost. That day he was in the yard, inspecting the front porch steps. He paused long enough to make silly faces at me, which made me laugh. To anyone else, it would have looked like I was shrieking gleefully at an empty yard, but Mom knew better. She'd wondered if I would have abilities like hers, and my reaction to Mr. Albertson proved I did. After that, she raised me to see ghosts as a normal part of life, although she'd emphasized that being able to see them was something special, and that I shouldn't broadcast my ability because not everyone would understand it.

I wasn't sure why I told Tim all that. It's not like I'm usually eager to outline all the ways I'm weird and freaky. He was just so genuinely interested that . . . I guess it made me feel sort of important. It was nice to share all that with someone without being ridiculed.

Still, now that my mom had come up, I was pretty sure I knew where the conversation was headed. I didn't want to talk about her, or the night she died, or anything like that, so I changed the subject. "So why doesn't Isobel like you?"

"Oh." He looked a little sheepish. "Isobel doesn't really like anyone. But me in particular . . . She doesn't like me because I'm a vampire."

Okay. What the heck was I supposed to say to that?

He continued immediately, saving me from the obligation of a quick reply. "Half vampire, really. But that still counts."

"Ha-ha. Counts. Vampire."

"I'm not kidding, Violet. I've always known I was . . . different."

"Haven't we all?" I wanted to point out that he didn't know what "different" was unless he too had gotten in trouble in kindergarten for insisting that the long-deceased teacher said it was okay to go to the bathroom. Mrs. Bloomington had once taught kindergarten at Palmetto Elementary, but she'd also been dead for over fifteen years. My current teacher had neither appreciated nor condoned my disappearing act and my excuse that her late predecessor had given me permission to leave the classroom. That was before I really understood that not only could most people not see ghosts, but that they didn't even believe they existed. And how was I to know that the authority of a living person outweighed a dead one?

"See, my dad left my mom before I was born," Tim said.

"Have you ever met him?"

"No. I used to ask Mom about him, and all she'd say was that he drained her dry, financially and emotionally. Then I saw this old Dracula movie on cable, and . . . I dunno. I guess my imagination kind of took over. Plus, I like rare hamburgers, and I can see pretty well in the dark, and I really hate garlic and sunlight."

"You were just in the sun half an hour ago, on the way home from the bus stop."

"Yeah, but I didn't like it."

"You weren't even wearing sunglasses!"

"I forgot them at home today."

I was tempted to tell him he was being ridiculous, but the thing was, I felt like I was the last person to chastise someone for their beliefs. I mean, hello? Paranormal communication? Pet poltergeist? Gemstones with protective properties? Did any of those sound more rational than Tim's Dracula Daddy theory?

I tried to remember other vampire legends. "Can you see yourself when you look in the mirror?"

"Yeah. But remember, I'm only half vampire."

"Can you turn into a bat?"

"No, but—"

"Half vampire. I know. You don't bite people and drink blood and stuff, do you?"

"I get kind of sick at the sight of blood," Tim said, looking slightly squirmy.

"Okay, so then why doesn't Isobel like you? She seems like the type who'd be really into the whole vampire thing."

Tim sighed a little. "Goths don't always like vampires. Plus she thinks I'm making it up. And she thinks I'm annoying." He picked at a loose thread on his arm warmer.

"So anyway, I told you about my dad, now tell me about your mom. Was she really a ghost hunter?"

Darn. Right back to this. "She was a paranormal investigator, yeah. She also did lectures, and she and Dad ran a website that sold investigative equipment and books." They'd made a great team—Mom was the intuitive, sympathetic one who sensed spirits and sought to help them, and Dad was the reformed skeptic determined to document significant scientific proof of his wife's experiences.

"And the cops really thought your dad killed her?"

That was my least favorite part of the whole mess, and I seriously didn't want to discuss it. Okay, so for about five minutes, the police thought Mom's death was a murder, and Dad was their chief suspect. I hated that people still remembered that so many years later. That's small-town living for you.

I gave Tim my most withering glare. "She fell down some stairs. That's it. Shut up, okay?"

"Sorry." He sunk down in his chair a little, looking appropriately scolded, but I could tell he was still curious.

Before he could start up with his interrogation again, though, the front door of the apartment opened and closed, and Dad came into the kitchen.

"Finished with Mrs. Wilson," he said. His shirtsleeves

were still rolled up to the elbows, and he smelled like a chem lab mixed with industrial-strength soap. "Now that I have a little more time, how was school?" he asked me.

"Well, I got teased because of your job, everyone thinks I'm a freak, and worst of all, I have to take gym." I motioned for Tim to follow me, and we went to hang out in my room.

On the way, I asked Tim if he'd taken any gym classes at Palmetto. The memory of the thing in the locker room was still lurking in my head, and I suddenly wondered if the presence stuck to the girls' room only, or if it haunted the boys' room, too. No way was I about to sneak in and see for myself, though. Ew.

He nodded. "Beginning Gym. Last year. It sucked."

"Yeah. Hey, did you ever notice anything weird in the locker room?" I didn't really think he'd be able to tell me much, but it was worth a try.

"Well, it usually smells weird in there," Tim said. He obviously had no idea what I was fishing for, but he wanted to be helpful.

So much for that.

"Don't they all?" I asked, rolling my eyes. "Hey, want to see Buster eat a cookie?"

CHAPTER FIVE
high school hell gate

That evening I couldn't stop thinking about school and the presence in the locker room. Maybe I'd overreacted. After all, I'd been stressed about gym, and anxiety can play all kinds of tricks—I certainly wasn't helpless when it came to spooky stuff. Mom had worked with all kinds of paranormal phenomena, and so could I. I knew she'd be really proud of me for dealing with this myself.

Besides, she'd always taught me that ghosts and stuff weren't really dangerous. You just had to figure out how to handle them, and the first step in doing that was figuring out who—or what—you were working with.

The only thing was, I'd never done a paranormal investigation before, and Mom hadn't told me much about them when I was little. I knew she and Dad had had all kinds of equipment, but if Dad still had any of it, I had no idea where it was or how it worked.

So I grabbed my laptop and searched the Internet for paranormal investigation techniques.

Along with all kinds of warnings that I pretty much ignored, I found plenty of information about equipment. Unfortunately, I didn't have access to things like digital thermometers or electromagnetic field detectors or fancy cameras. I did have the digital camera on my phone, though, and I also had an app for recording sound bites. I thought that would work well enough as a digital voice recorder. Photos might give me proof of spirit activity, and recordings could give me something called EVP— electronic voice phenomena. According to my reading, it seemed like ghostly noises that weren't audible in person sometimes came through in recordings.

The trick would be finding a way to conduct the investigation at a time when the locker room wasn't full of girls dressing for gym. For that, I'd have to be a little sneaky. Like I said, sometimes you've got to break a few rules when you're dealing with ghosts.

The next morning in the locker room, I changed clothes as fast as possible, while the blood pounded in my ears and that horrible rage constricted around me. I slipped my phone into the pocket of my gym shorts, stuffed my regular clothes and bag into my locker, and skidded into the gym at full speed. I wasn't ready to go back in the locker room yet. I wasn't, I wasn't, I wasn't. Maybe I'd just stay out here and . . .

Then I saw Coach Frucile and several students setting up a volleyball net. Hmm, which was worse: the wheezing evil in the locker room or volleyball?

Considering my habit of getting hit in the head by gym equipment, I figured it was a tie.

At least I lucked out—my team wasn't among the first to play, so we sat on the bleachers and watched while two other teams struggled on the court. Coach Frucile was focused on the game, yelling out instructions and corrections and insults I assumed were supposed to be encouraging. She wasn't paying any attention to the bleachers at all, so after a few minutes I was able to slide off my seat and slip out into the side hall. From there, I took a deep breath, steadied myself, and headed back into the locker room.

The thing swelled around me again immediately, all sorrow and anger and invisible darkness, a fog bank of unrest. It dripped out from the showers and filled the room, silent and creeping, as heavy and drifting as an approaching thunderstorm. Fighting against it, I pulled out my phone and started snapping photos of the room around me. I couldn't see anything on my phone's tiny screen, but later I would transfer the pictures to my computer and blow them up to study them more closely.

The air pulsed, physically pushing me. Although everything looked still, I felt like I was fighting the winds of a hurricane. Hot spots turned into cold spots, then back again. I went from sweating to shivering.

The pressure in my head was starting to blur my vision again. I switched to the recorder app and tried to talk to the thing. According to what I'd read online, I was supposed to ask questions, then wait for answers that might not be audible until I played the recording back.

"Who are you?" I asked. I was yelling, but the blood pounding in my ears drowned out even the sound of my own voice. "What do you want? Is there something you need help with? Something that would let you move on?"

Then I looked down at the phone. Its screen was blank; it had turned off. I tried to turn it back on, but nothing happened. It was dead.

So much for getting EVP.

Suddenly something wrenched the phone from my fingers and flung it across the room, into the shower alcove. The overhead lights flickered, and unlocked locker doors began to open and slam shut repeatedly. A first aid kit bolted to the wall near Coach Frucile's office shuddered and fell open, spilling bandages and antibacterial wipes and disposable cold packs onto the floor. I pressed my back against the end of one bank of lockers.

"You can't hurt me!" I yelled as invisible winds whipped around me, pulling at me, dragging me toward the alcove.

Then the thing's intensity pulled back a little, just enough for me to notice Coach Frucile watching me from the doorway.

"Um," I said, breathing hard.

"Forget your inhaler again?"

"Kind of."

"Get back in here. Your team's up. If I catch you leaving my class again, it'll be a week of detention. Got it?"

"Got it," I muttered. To tell the truth, I was so glad to get away from the thing that I almost welcomed the idea of volleyball—until I took my first ball to the forehead, anyway. I wondered how much of my encounter Coach Frucile had witnessed. Had she heard me yelling? Had she seen the lockers opening and shutting on their own? Had she wondered why the first aid kit's contents were all over the floor? If she had, she gave no sign.

I managed to find my phone when I reluctantly returned to the locker room to change after class. Despite having been tossed around, it worked just fine once I got it out of the locker room. None of the photos or recordings I'd gotten were on the memory card, though.

After that, I started going to school in my gym

clothes, with my regular clothes crammed into my messenger bag. When first period ended, I changed in the bathroom. Anything to avoid the locker room. I felt unsafe in there.

Drawing was better, since I had Tim to talk to. But Head Jock (technically Jake Bartle, though I preferred my own nickname for him) and his minions were still upset about the Dirk thing, so they looked for any excuse to give me a hard time.

They had even started calling me "Spookygirl." I suppose it could have been worse—Spookygirl sounded kind of cool, like a superhero name. And at least it kept the jocks from picking on Tim, which had apparently been the status quo before my arrival. I even encouraged the attention, reporting on Dirk's activities whenever he was spooking around.

"He's laughing at your drawing," I told Head Jock when Dirk leaned over his drawing bench and guffawed at Head Jock's lopsided attempt at a still life in charcoal.

Dirk gave me a misty blue glare. "Freakin' quit it, will you?"

"Yeah, right," said Head Jock, but he glanced nervously over his shoulder anyway. "If you really can see dead people, tell me what my grandpa's first name was."

It was one of the dumbest ghost-related demands I'd ever heard. I wasn't psychic—unless Head Jock's dead grandfather was following him around and happened to introduce himself, there was no way I could know his name. Still, I figured Head Jock was trying to mess with me, so I took a guess and went with the obvious. "Your grandpa's not dead."

Head Jock's left eye twitched amusingly. "How'd you know?"

I rolled my eyes. "Dirk told me."

"Spookygirl," Head Jock muttered, returning to his still life. On the paper in front of him, a pitcher drooped hopelessly next to an apple that looked more like a horribly damaged internal organ. A kidney, maybe.

"Hey." Dead Dirk vanished from next to Head Jock's bench and reappeared next to me. The temperature around us dropped a few degrees. It wasn't really noticeable unless you knew a ghost was nearby—nothing like what happened when Buster was around. "How come you keep doing that?"

Crap. I hated moments like this, when ghosts wanted to chitchat in public. I'd more than learned my lesson in the hall with Henry on the first day of school.

"Not a good time," I muttered, trying not to move my mouth.

"Did you say something?" Tim muttered back.

I shook my head.

Dirk didn't give up. "I'm serious. Why do you keep telling my friends I'm still here?"

"Uh, because you *are*," I said. "Why do you care?"

"It's freaking them out."

"Well, they deserve it. They're jerks."

"Yeah, but . . ." Dead Dirk didn't have an argument for that, so he scowled at me, called me Spookygirl, and disappeared. That was rich—being called spooky by a freakin' ghost. Pot, meet kettle.

Tim poked me in the arm with his charcoal, leaving a black smudge near my elbow. "You *were* talking to someone. And it got a little cold. Was that a ghost? Was it Dirk Reynolds?"

"Yeah." I went back to drawing my pitcher and apple—which, unlike Head Jock's, actually looked like a pitcher and an apple. "He wasn't the sharpest crayon in the box, was he?"

"He didn't need to be." Tim had traded his striped arm warmers for a set of leather wrist cuffs, and he wore what looked like a cheap black dog collar around his neck. The sunglasses he'd forgotten the first day of school were perched on top of his head—he'd tried a few times to keep them on during class, but Mr. Connelly insisted otherwise. Tim squinted (when he remembered to) as the early afternoon sunlight poured through the windows. "Dirk was a star athlete," he went on. "He set, like, a million records when he played for Palmetto."

"Even though he was only a junior when he died?"

"Yeah. The senior players hated him for it."

"And how'd he die? A car wreck?"

"Yeah. He was drinking at a party, and he tried to drive home. Why?"

"That sucks."

I'd thought maybe he was secretly murdered by a football rival. It would explain why he was still hanging around. But no, he was just another tragic high school movie-of-the-week cliché. "Then why is he still hanging around with these clowns?"

Tim shrugged. "These guys were freshmen then. They idolized Dirk. Maybe he still wants adoring fans."

That was just shallow enough to make sense.

"Six minutes until the bell," Mr. Connelly said. "Let's wrap it up, people."

After finishing my drawing, I glanced up to where Head Jock continued to struggle with his still life. The lopsided pitcher now looked like an abstract dead fish, and the kidney-apple had exploded. It hit me that Head Jock was probably having about as much fun getting his art requirement out of the way as I was having with my gym requirement.

Well, it was only fair.

At home that afternoon, Tim watched as I dumped my gym clothes out of my bag and smoothed them out so they'd look okay in the morning.

"Why don't you just leave those in your locker?" he asked.

I'd never told him about any of the locker-room stuff, but he'd helped me out with a little of Dirk's history, so maybe he'd know some elements of Palmetto High history as well. "This is gonna sound weird, but are there any school legends or rumors about something terrible happening in the girls' locker room?"

"You mean besides those awful gym clothes?" He poked at the yellow-and-green monstrosities on my bed.

"I'm serious." I told him about what I'd experienced, and why I couldn't go back.

"I've never heard about anything. What do you think it is? I mean, if a bunch of girls got stabbed to death in there or something, you'd think people would know."

"It feels like something like that," I sighed. "Or something worse."

We spent the next hour searching online for old news articles about Palmetto High and murders, but we didn't find anything.

"Maybe it was covered up," Tim suggested. "Maybe nobody knows it ever happened."

I shuddered.

"This thing really bothers you, doesn't it?"

I wanted to get defensive and say no, but I guessed my habit of changing clothes in the bathroom made the truth pretty obvious.

"Yeah. That's not usually the case, but this is so different from anything I've ever felt. I can't believe nobody else notices it."

"Well, maybe you're more sensitive than most people. And you've told me ghosts get more active when you're around, so maybe it only happens when you're in the room."

"Lucky me. But what about Coach Frucile? She spends more time in there than anyone. Her office is in there! How can she just sit there and not go nuts?"

Tim's eyes widened. "Maybe she knows about it, but it doesn't go after her."

"What? It's like her very own Buster or something?"

"I don't know. Maybe she was in on the murders and everything. Maybe she's at the center of the whole thing!"

"I doubt it," I said, but then I thought about the coldness in Coach Frucile's eyes.

"Let's look her up. What's her first name?"

"Um . . ." I dug through the pile of papers on my desk, looking for the class syllabus Coach Frucile had distributed on the first day of school; it included contact information like her full name and office phone number. "Lilith."

"And how do you spell Frucile?" He typed as I spelled. Then he sat back and studied her name in the search bar.

"You're supposed to hit return for the search to work," I said drily.

"Shut up. There's something . . . Don't you see anything weird about her name?"

"Not really."

"Frucile. It just sounds weird. And look, if you rearrange the letters . . ." He typed another word beside Frucile in the search box. Lucifer.

"What are you trying to say?"

"That your gym teacher's evil?"

"We already established that. Her name could be Mother Teresa and she'd still be evil."

"But don't you think it's strange? And look at her first name. Lilith. Lilith was a demon in a couple of ancient mythologies. She drank blood."

"Why am I not surprised you know that? Whatever, I'm sure it's just a coincidence."

"But you don't know that." Tim continued. "What kinds of things do you feel in the locker room? Maybe we'd be better off researching what you're experiencing."

That was good paranormal-investigation reasoning, and I wished I'd thought of it. I started describing what I'd felt, and Tim typed the words into the search box. The list we ended up with included *evil presence*, *threatening*, *haunted*, *heat*, *cold*, and *things moving by themselves*. When he hit search, the first site on the list of results was that of a paranormal investigation society in Oregon. Their archives included an account of a reported haunting that turned out to be something else entirely; after investigating, the society's members suspected they were dealing with a portal of evil. "If there's such a thing as Hell," the report said, "we just found its servants' entrance."

The possibility traced down my spine like an icy finger.

"Did your parents ever investigate anything like this?" Tim asked.

"I don't know. Dad won't talk about any of it. But Mom used to tell me she was never really afraid during investigations, and this sounds like it would scare anyone."

The report, which identified the investigated property as a building on Ramsay Court in an unspecified city, described elements that were all too familiar—hot and cold spots, objects moving on their own, a heavy and overwhelming sense of doom. After cutting short their initial visit, the investigators refused to go back; they recommended the property owners seek help from religious groups or experienced psychics. "The entities entering and leaving through the portal were demonic in nature, and more powerful than we were equipped to measure or deal with," the report summarized.

The more I thought about it, the more it seemed like the girls' locker room was as appropriate a place as any for a hell gate.

The report also explained that the Ramsay Court property had been abandoned for years; inside, the investigators found evidence of possible demonic rituals, including "black candles, symbols drawn on the walls and floor, drops of what appeared to be dried blood. It may have been an organized ritual meant to create a doorway or call forth a demon. Or it may have been a couple of kids trespassing and playing around, inadvertently opening a gateway."

Another part of the report mentioned the tests the investigators performed and the measurements they took before the investigation was aborted. Most of the group's equipment malfunctioned early on—flashlights with fresh batteries stopped working near the portal, only to "fix" themselves later on. Two digital cameras did the same. A film camera appeared to work, but the resulting negatives were blank. The tape inside an analog recorder snapped.

"Kind of like my phone," I said to Tim as we read.

But some of the equipment worked long enough to produce results. A digital recorder picked up a hiss which had caused some debate among the society members— some wanted to consider it EVP, but the majority disagreed because no discernable voices could be heard in the static.

A sample of the sound was available for download; it sounded like a radio stuck between stations. "Digital enhancement of the hiss does not reveal any real hint of EVP, or electronic voice phenomena," the report noted. "In a 'normal' haunting, we would expect to find evidence of EVP. The lack of recognizable EVP was one factor that led us to believe the entities encountered in the Ramsay Court property were not human in origin, but were instead entering our world through some sort of portal located within the house." The investigators also recorded elevated magnetic fields and noticeable temperature fluctuations in several rooms.

The team members agreed that the entities in the Ramsay Court property were unlike anything they'd encountered before. One member was so spooked that she dropped out of the society after the investigation and refused to discuss her experience or contribute to the account.

"Oh man," Tim said when he finished reading. "This is too cool."

"Are you kidding? You're scared of Buster, but you think a hell gate is cool."

"I'm not scared of Buster anymore."

"Then why do you always make me lead the way around the apartment?"

He scowled a little. "Come on! Demonic rituals opening up portals of evil? Maybe something like that's going on in our school right now!"

I frowned. "It's not cool at all. This is why people shouldn't play around with things they don't understand." The idea was making me more and more uncomfortable. I remembered Mom explaining when I was little that people who didn't really believe in ghosts and whatever were the most likely to stir up trouble with things like Ouija boards and séances. Even with friendly, harmless ghosts, you had to know what you were doing.

"Maybe Coach Lucifer's behind the whole thing."

"Whatever." I didn't want to think about Frucile holding some kind of midnight ritual in the locker room.

"I'm serious. You said everything seems to come out of the shower stalls, right? Think about it—if you were conducting a bloody ritual, you'd want to do it somewhere that would be easy to clean, right? You just turn on the water, and whoosh, the evidence goes right down the drain. You'd need one of those black light things they have on cop shows to see the residue."

"And with a little bleach," I mused, "even that would be gone."

"So then why is it impossible that Coach Lucifer might be, I don't know, holding sacrifices in there?"

81

"Because the idea is nuts." In truth, it was starting to seem way more plausible than I wanted it to. "And just what do you think she's sacrificing?"

"I dunno. Chickens? Stray cats? Students who forget their gym clothes?" Tim was getting way too into this theory. "We do get those announcements about runaways pretty regularly. Someone seems to disappear every few months, and we don't always hear that they've been found. Maybe . . ."

"Maybe they just ran away," I finished for him. "What would Frucile do with the bodies after these sacrifices? Stuff *them* down the shower drains, too?"

"Okay, I was exaggerating. But something could be going on, and that's why you were feeling all that weird stuff. You can't still think the Frucile-Lucifer thing's just a coincidence. The name's obviously made up. Hey!" He stood up, excitedly. "Does your dad still have his old ghost hunting equipment?"

"I don't know. I assume he got rid of it. He's so not into that anymore."

"You should find out. And if he still has it, maybe you can sneak some of it into the locker room and see if you find any magnetic fields, or those electric-phenom-thingies—"

"Electronic voice phenomena," I said.

"Yeah, those."

"The Ramsay Court investigators didn't find any EVP."

"Then if you get some, you'll know you might be dealing with a haunting instead of a portal. Either way, holy crap. Palmetto just got a lot more interesting."

"No way." I shook my head. "I'm not going back in that room. That thing didn't want me there."

"Or maybe it did," Tim said slowly. "You said it was pulling you toward the showers, right?"

"Yeah."

"And Coach Frucile gave you a weird look after that."

"She's given me several weird looks."

"So what if the thing in the locker room wants you? What if you're the next sacrifice?"

"Tim, that's so not funny." Problem was, I wasn't entirely sure he was trying to be funny at all.

The thought burrowed into the back of my mind and stayed there. What if he was on the right track, and the reason only I could feel the thing so strongly was because it was focusing on me? Staying out of the locker room seemed smarter than ever.

But one other thing kept bugging me. Mom wouldn't have been scared of this. She might have seen it as a challenge, but she wouldn't have run away. She would have researched and investigated until she figured out what was going on and put a stop to it. Which meant I had to do the same.

CHAPTER SIX
guinea pig poltergeist

Considering how Dad felt about anything ghost-related, I couldn't very well just ask him about his old paranormal investigation equipment. Instead, I made a list of all the places in the apartment where he might've stashed it—and since the apartment was small, my list was short. I didn't dare snoop through his stuff while he was around, but whenever he was out chauffeuring corpses in the funeral home's hearse, I hit one of the spots on the list.

I didn't find anything in his closet or dresser, or in the storage bins under his bed. There was no equipment hidden in the hall closet or the television cabinet, either. I even searched my own room, hoping he might've stored the stuff in a forgotten corner of the closet back when he was using the room as his office. Nothing.

After I'd exhausted all the possibilities in the apartment, I redirected my hunt and started poking around downstairs. Nothing turned up in Dad's office. I couldn't get into one of the cabinets in the embalming room, so guiltily, I filched the key from Dad's briefcase. All I found were jugs of chemicals. There was still the spare room to check, but it was empty except for a couple of coffins—all discontinued floor models. Dad intended to sell them off at a discount, but he hadn't gotten around to it yet.

Coffins. Human-sized storage boxes, essentially. The very place to hide those mementos you'd rather forget about . . .

I couldn't have thought of this a little sooner?

The coffins were dusty, and they showed assorted scratches and dents from the time they'd spent on display. Two were empty. But when I lifted the curved top half of the third coffin's lid, I found some battered cardboard boxes taped shut and nestled on the faded satin. *Robin* had been scrawled on the top of each box, in thick black permanent ink, in Dad's handwriting.

Okay, score. Even though the equipment had been Dad's specialty, it made sense that he might have packed it away with the rest of his memories of Mom.

And tossed it all in a coffin. And people think *I'm* morbid.

I had to work fast. I expected Dad home within half an hour. That wasn't enough time to go through the boxes, and I couldn't let him find me snooping in the spare room. I wanted to grab all the boxes at once, but since there wasn't enough space in my tiny bedroom to store them all, I'd have to settle for attacking them one at a time. I could sort through the first one, then trade it for another the next time Dad was out. I tucked a box under my arm, closed the coffin, and ran back up to the apartment.

I figured the boxes couldn't all contain equipment. There were probably all kinds of clues and stuff in them. The idea of finding out more about Mom excited me a lot more than investigating the shower room hell gate.

I opened the top flaps and found a scattered mess of papers, photographs, and assorted little things. It looked like everything had been packed quickly, without any attempt at organization.

It was how I'd pack away the belongings and mementos of a loved one I'd just lost. I bet Dad had stuffed everything of emotional value in these boxes, and he probably hadn't opened them since. At least he had kept them, but why hang onto a bunch of memories you won't let yourself enjoy or remember? Sure Mom was dead, but the contents of the boxes might've let us feel closer to her all these years.

I came across Mom's address book, small and lavender, with a pair of cartoon owls on the cover. I remembered those owls. When I was little, Mom always made sure I wrote thank-you notes for any presents I got from friends and relatives (even Aunt Thelma, who always gave awful, useful presents like socks and savings bonds). When I had a note ready to send, Mom would tell me to look up the address in her little book.

I found a drawing of a black cat I'd scribbled for her when I was five. I'd wanted a cat in the worst way back then, but Mom didn't think it would be wise to trust Buster with small animals. She was afraid he'd get jealous and do something . . . unappealing to them.

Then I found a tangled clutter of stuff that looked like it had come straight from the top of a dresser. Dad had probably swiped it all into the box at once, just so he wouldn't have to look at it. A silver chain, a couple of movie ticket stubs and receipts, a really ancient tube of peppermint lip balm, a single earring, a pen, a ponytail holder, a small wooden jewelry box, some change. And a single gemstone—a tiger's eye, shiny and smooth. I remembered that stone, remembered admiring it. Mom hadn't carried it around with her, but she kept it because she thought the brown tones were pretty. I liked the way the textures shimmered and shifted when I rolled the stone in my palm.

Dad had told me Mom's things were gone. It was really hard not to be mad at him for keeping the boxes a secret; finding just a few small things gave me back parts of Mom I thought I'd lost.

Under a to-do list and a couple of bank statements,

I found a small, box-shaped object made of black plastic. It looked a little like an old television remote, only with knobs instead of buttons, and a dark digital screen. Okay, this had to be something important. There was a power switch on the side; I turned it on, but nothing happened. I flipped the box over and saw a battery compartment on the back. From the box's weight, I guessed there were probably dead batteries inside. *Please tell me they didn't leak,* I thought, opening the compartment. I was in luck.

After changing the batteries, I tried the power switch again. This time the digital readout lit up in bright green. A second later it registered a 1.4, whatever that meant. I'd need to research how to use it, but from what I'd read in the Ramsay Court account, I guessed it was probably an EMF reader, a device that measured electromagnetic fields. The presence of a ghost was supposed to cause a surge in the reading. There was only one sure way to test that theory.

"Buster!"

I heard an unholy squeal rattle from the direction of the living room. Seconds later the temperature in my room dropped. Buster screeched with joy, levitated my pillow, and hit me on the head with it. Before getting bopped by my poltergeist, I saw the EMF readout change. The number went crazy, spiking up to 18.9, then wavering back and forth between that and 12.3 as Buster moved around the room.

Buster picked up the pillow again; like a girl on a sugar high at a slumber party, he used it to whack me on the shoulder a couple of times. I did my best to ignore the smacks and watched the meter.

"Okay, Buster. Wanna play? Go get your toy. Get your squeaky burger!"

With a delighted cry, Buster left the room. The temperature returned to normal; the EMF reading settled back down to 1.4.

It worked.

A moment later, the rubber hamburger sailed into the room and landed on my lap.

Buster reentered the room with a squeal, and the reading went back up. This was way too awesome.

I switched off the detector, then squeaked the burger and threw it into the hall. "Go get it!"

Soon it flew back into the room and bounced off my arm. Buster made one of his unearthly chuckling noises.

I could hear Dad downstairs; it sounded like he'd just gotten home. I put the reader back in the box and crammed the whole thing into a dresser drawer, carefully hidden under a couple of shirts. Then, to thank Buster for being so helpful, I played fetch for a few more minutes and rewarded him with a cookie. Overcome with happiness, he screamed and pulled my hair.

* * *

Over the next week, I went through the rest of the boxes and unearthed a scientific digital thermometer, a motion detector, and a sound recorder. Everything was years out of date, technologically speaking, but it would do. In exchange for attention and cookies, Buster was my willing guinea pig for each. The thermometer registered the temperature fluctuations that occurred around him, and the sound recorder picked up his cries and squeals clearly. He was a loud ghost, though; even people without abilities like mine could hear him. I wondered how the recorder would do in the locker room, if it could pick up any EVP.

The motion detector did absolutely nothing, even when I riled Buster up. It only detected movement when he levitated or threw a solid object, but even then, it only registered the floating item, not Buster. He was invisible, even to me. Maybe the detector would work better on the kind of ghost I could see. Not that I thought I'd have luck with it in the locker room, anyway—I needed tools that could take fast readings, like the temperature gauge and the EMF reader. I sure as hell wasn't going to sit around for hours and wait for the motion detector to go off.

I had hoped to find a camera with some kind of infrared feature, or maybe a film camera, but nothing turned up. My own digital camera would have to do if I couldn't locate anything better. I'd just have to hope for orbs or weird spectral mists.

I also found lots of Mom's personal stuff during my search. Some of it, like the address book and the tiger's eye, I kept out of the boxes and hid away in my room. I kept some of her jewelry, too—the silver chain, a pendant made from a shard of obsidian, a ring embedded with tiny crystal chips, and a rose quartz necklace. I couldn't wear any of it and risk Dad recognizing it, so I hoarded it away in Mom's wooden jewelry box and tucked everything into a nightstand drawer. I kept my own jewelry in the box as well—the spider earrings and the various purple bracelets and rings I'd collected.

But even though I was thrilled to find so many of Mom's things, it wasn't until I opened the last box that I realized what I had really been searching for.

The box held a stack of file folders, and each folder represented a different ghost hunt. All of Mom's notes and research were there: the pre-investigation interviews the team had conducted, the measurements they'd taken, and Mom's post-investigation accounts. I wanted to read everything; I paged through file after file. Reading Mom's notes and reports was almost like having her peeking over my shoulder, telling me more about how each investigation had progressed.

Then I came across a folder I wasn't sure I was ready to read: the Logan Street file. It was unfinished and disorganized, and that seemed really wrong. Mom was so meticulous about arranging the elements of each investigation, but the Logan Street notes were jumbled and messy, and, of course, there was no final write-up.

A strange thought hit me then. Maybe I could finish it—I could look over Mom's research, add a little of my own, and, based on what I found and what I already knew, write an account of the investigation for the folder. It would be difficult, but I knew Mom would appreciate the effort, and it might even provide some closure. Plus, I really wanted to learn as much as I could about that night. I still only had a skeleton of an idea of what had happened on Riley Island.

According to Mom's notes, the Logan Street property had been bought and sold a number of times over the years. Each new owner thought he had gotten a deal until he or his family spent the night. The weird thing was how different each experience seemed to be. The men usually noticed some pretty typical paranormal activity—strange noises, cold spots, stuff like that. But the women heard whispered threats and sometimes got manhandled by invisible beings. I'm not even kidding—one woman said she felt someone grab her arm and wrench her toward the main staircase. Even the local historical society had refused to accept the house as a donation and take ownership of it after one of their female representatives had a bad experience there.

Mom had suspected the house was haunted by the

ghosts of James Riley, Jr., and his wife, Abigail, who both died on the same night back in 1932. She hadn't been able to find more information than that; the local historical archive's old headquarters had flooded during a hurricane in the 1960s, and a lot of the early history of Riley Island had been lost.

I figured I could research Riley Island online, and hopefully find some historical details Mom hadn't been able to uncover. And maybe I could even use Mom's address book to track down the other members of Palmetto Paranormal and see if they could tell me anything about the night of the investigation. The idea of contacting Mom's old friend Sabrina Brightstar didn't exactly thrill me, but I needed all the firsthand accounts I could get. Anything to learn more about that night.

Unfortunately, though, officially reopening the Logan Street file would have to wait until after the locker-room investigation. I had to face whatever was in there head-on, and soon, especially if Tim was right and it had some kind of weird interest in me. I'd send that thing packing, and then I'd have one less thing to worry about. And maybe I could even stop dragging my gym clothes home with me every day.

CHAPTER SEVEN
who ya gonna call?

Since I'd been disgusted by the overcrowded cafeteria, I did at Palmetto what I'd done at Lakewood—I started hiding in the library. As it turns out, a high school library can be a safe haven from many things besides greasy food and obnoxious peers: nagging teachers, assemblies, pep rallies. Yeah, especially that last one. Noisy, boring, stupid things where cheerleaders jump around and some guy in a mascot costume acts like an idiot and everyone yells and screams a lot, and you're supposed to care and "show school spirit."

Show school spirit? No thanks. I had enough school spirits to deal with already.

By the time the first pep rally of the year came around, Miss Walters, the head librarian, and I were old buddies. It wasn't hard to get on her good side—I offered to help shelve books a few times, and once I proved that I understood the Dewey Decimal System—it's not that complicated!—she adored me.

Pep rallies were always held during the last period of the day, so it was easy for me and Tim to sneak away together after drawing class. Technically, attendance at pep rallies was mandatory for the entire student body; when Miss Walters saw me, though, she waved me inside.

"Sit near the back so Mr. Stoltz won't see you if he peeks in," she said. Mr. Stoltz, the troll-like vice principal and dean of discipline, loved ferreting out anyone who dared to default on his or her school spirit.

Tim and I sat at a small study table, the view of which was blocked from the library's entrance by a couple of bookshelves.

"So have you decided yet?" he asked.

I was too distracted to figure out what he was asking. Earlier that day, Ms. Geller had assigned our midterm English project—a descriptive essay about our most vivid childhood memory—and I couldn't stop thinking about it. She was giving us plenty of time, she said, because she wanted us to put a lot of thought into our essays and turn in something meaningful and full of concrete detail. Her expectations were high, and the essay would count for a quarter of our semester grade.

Great. My most vivid childhood memory was the night my mom died. No way was I writing about that. Finishing Mom's Riley Island file was one thing, but I wasn't about to yack about her death in an English essay. That night was no one else's business, and the thought of putting it down on paper for my teacher to read was enough to make me moody. I'd think of another memory. Or I'd make one up.

Tim gave me a look, and I realized he was still waiting for an answer.

"Sorry. Decided what?"

"How you're going to do the ghost hunt. The investigation."

"Not yet. I need to get in while the locker room's empty, and I can't risk just sneaking in again. Coach Frucile keeps an eye on me now." Ever since I'd shown Tim the equipment I'd unearthed, he'd been dying to know when I was going to investigate the presence—and he wanted to help. However, I didn't know how to get myself, let alone a boy, into the girls' locker room when I wasn't supposed to be there. My inhaler excuse had gone stale.

"Fake an injury during gym."

"Like I need to fake them." We'd moved on to the track unit by then, and track was nearly as unlucky for me as volleyball. I had already skinned my knee at the end of one class, and . . . Something wiggled in my mind. "The first aid kit." The one on the wall near Coach Frucile's office. She'd gone into the locker room to get me a bandage while I hovered outside. "Wait, that might work."

"What about the first aid kit?" Tim was practically bouncing in his chair. He had bleached a white streak in his hair the week before, then dyed it with lime Kool-Aid. It was now a sickly swamp green, and it flopped over his forehead when he moved.

"You know those cold packs you activate by bending?" I said. "There are a few of those in the kit. If I pretend to twist my ankle or something during class, maybe she'd let me hobble to the locker room to get one."

"Wouldn't she just send someone else to get it for you?"

"Oh." Shoot. "I guess."

Tim's eyebrows arched up evilly. "You need someone else to fall. Then you could be the one running for the first aid kit."

"Hmm. Wouldn't it be a shame if that happened?" Not that I really wanted anyone to get hurt, but sometimes a good investigation requires a little sacrifice. I tented my fingers under my chin and began to consider the candidates.

And so it was that the next morning, while several of my classmates prepped for a four-lap relay race, I *accidentally* nudged my foot over the painted line and into the first lane of the track. Gosh, how careless of me. Christy Palmer's toes caught on the edge of my sensible white gym sneaker, and she went sprawling onto the hot asphalt with a scream.

Whoops.

"Omigod!" I said, feigning concern as she rolled over

and sat up. Actually, I really was a little concerned. She'd gone down harder than I'd expected—I figured she'd, you know, at least *try* to catch herself—and she'd bumped her knee pretty hard. I had nothing against mousy Christy and her owl-eyed glasses, and I hoped her injury wasn't too bad. On the bright side, a badly bruised, scraped-up knee was as good an excuse as any for me to fetch the first aid kit. I got Christy up and helped her to the nearest bench while Coach Frucile hurried over. When I offered to get the kit, Coach Frucile was too concerned about Christy (and the school's liability, I figured) to notice I'd suddenly turned into Little Miss Helpful.

I only had a few minutes to work before Coach Frucile would wonder where I was. I stopped quickly at my regular locker for my messenger bag, which held my equipment. Then I headed to the locker room. On the way in I almost smacked into Tim, who was skulking around its entrance like a kid working up the nerve to shoplift a candy bar from the drugstore.

"I skipped out of English," he said, holding up a bathroom pass.

I shushed him and peeked into the locker room. When I was sure it was empty, I motioned for him to follow as far as the doorway. "How long have you been here?"

"Ten minutes."

"Your teacher's going to think you have some kind of horrible problem."

He shrugged. "If she asks, I'll tell her I went out for Mexican food last night and the refried beans tasted weird. I don't think she'll want more info than that."

I took a few steps into the locker room, and the feeling closed around me. It smacked at me in pulsing waves, and this time, my vision almost seemed to redden, as if the surfaces of the room were all coated with a thin veneer of blood. That creepy feeling of being watched made the back of my neck prickle.

"So when's the scary stuff start?" Tim asked, lingering near the door and glancing in toward the shower alcove.

"You don't feel that?" The room itself felt alive and angry, with a bloody heat thudding against the walls of the shower.

He looked a little disappointed. "No."

There wasn't time to discuss it—but was it just my imagination, or did the feeling seem a little less fierce and heavy than usual? Maybe because I had a friend with me? I handed Tim a notebook and a pencil. "Write down whatever measurements I read off. I'll tell you what they mean later." He stuck close behind as I began to make my way through the room.

I started with the EMF reader. The readings I got

were bizarre: 14.6 near the main bank of lockers; a comparatively low 2.9 outside Coach Frucile's closed office door. At the entrance to the showers, the reading spiked to an incredible 31.3. The thing roared silently around me, shoving me toward the alcove. I nearly took a step inside; my sneaker was about to touch the tile floor when the EMF reader's screen went dark. It wouldn't turn back on.

I switched to the digital thermometer, but it was also dead. Despite the fact that I stood in a hot spot, I shivered.

"Do you feel that?" I asked Tim. "Feel how warm it is here?"

"I figured the air conditioner needed some work," he said.

"It's like a thousand degrees here." I stood still and stared into the alcove. A dark, almost palpable misery emanated from within, wrapping around me. It pulled at me and made me want to weep along with it.

But no—whatever this was, it couldn't have me. I thought of my mom and summoned up strength I didn't know I had, and I stepped away from the showers and pulled myself together. After a few seconds, I put the dead thermometer away, trading it for the digital recorder, which recorded for about thirty seconds before it, too, went dark. I also took a few quick shots with my digital camera, including one pointing directly into the shower alcove. Then I shoved everything back in my bag—Tim said he'd stick my things in his locker until fifth period—grabbed the first aid kit, and sprinted to the track. I figured I'd been gone for no more than fifteen minutes, tops.

"What took you so long?" Coach Frucile asked, but she didn't wait for an answer. Her concern and attention were still focused on Christy's knee, which was turning an almost pretty shade of purple.

I couldn't concentrate for the rest of the day. Even drawing class was torture, despite the fact that we were finally studying portraiture. Because of all my funeral home practice over the summer, I was looking forward to this unit. Plus, Mr. Connelly had chosen Cherry Cheerleader to serve as our model that day. Cherry looked really uncomfortable as Mr. Connelly described the principles of facial proportion and symmetry and pointed out all the ways her features didn't match the classical ideals. Any other day, Tim and I would've snickered endlessly as the various imperfections of one of our least favorite classmates were outlined. Today, though, we were both too antsy to savor the moment.

I did happen to notice, however, that Dead Dirk was there—he sat on an empty bench with a translucent blue drawing board balanced on his lap. He looked as if he were drawing Cherry right along with everyone else.

While I worked on my own drawing, I took a moment now and then to enjoy Head Jock's attempt at Cherry's portrait. He mixed up a few proportions and gave her a round face with tiny pig eyes and a monstrous, bulbous forehead. Then, as if he were drawing caricatures at a theme park, he added a tiny stick figure body with giant, lopsided boobs. His fellow jocks chuckled until Cherry lost her patience and stomped over from her perch in front of the class. When she saw Head Jock's drawing, she lost it and screamed.

"Babe, it's funny!" Head Jock said.

"Model, please!" Mr. Connelly clapped his hands the way he always did when he wanted someone's attention. "We don't want to move around and disrupt everyone's concentration, do we?"

Cherry appeared as though she very much wanted to disrupt something on Head Jock. If looks could kill, he might've ended up just as dead as Dirk.

Mr. Connelly continued. "Remember, Cherry, your grade for today depends on how well you follow directions as a model. Everyone's work depends on you."

Cherry whipped around and stalked back to the front of the room, where she sat fuming.

I raised my hand. "Mr. Connelly? Could you tell

Cherry to stop scowling like that? She has a lot more wrinkles on her forehead when she makes that face, and the change is messing up my portrait."

"If you please, Cherry," Mr. Connelly said. "Try a more neutral expression."

Cherry's eyes shot a few daggers at me before she relaxed her face, her expression reverting to its usual blankness.

That afternoon, Tim came home on the bus with me and we went up to my room to analyze the results of the investigation. While we waited for my computer to boot up and the photos to upload, I called Buster in to demonstrate some of the other instruments for Tim.

Tim still wasn't too sure how to coexist with Buster, and Buster dealt with this the way a cat deals with a dog person—Tim was his new favorite. He pranked Tim at every opportunity. My pillows or stuffed animals went flying without warning at Tim's head, and the television kept clicking on (and off) at full volume. Sometimes Tim whirled around as if he'd been tapped on the shoulder, but there was never anyone—anyone visible, anyway—behind him. It was enough to make anyone jumpy, so I usually intervened and threatened Buster with the crate, at which point he would retreat to another part of the apartment to sulk and wail.

But when I needed to demonstrate how something like an EMF reader worked in the presence of the paranormal, Buster was useful to have around. Luckily, the reader turned on and worked perfectly now that it was away from the locker room. I showed Tim the readout's fluctuations as Buster moved about.

"How come Buster doesn't make it malfunction like the thing in the locker room did?"

Truthfully, I didn't know, but I was getting there. "Well, I don't think there are rules to any of this. There's no normal. No two ghosts are going to behave exactly the same, so maybe they all manipulate energy in different ways." It was as good an explanation as any.

I tossed Buster's squeaky toy to send him on his way, then started looking through the notes Tim had taken in the locker room. "Look at these EMF readings—31.3 near the showers! That's ten points higher than anything I've gotten from Buster. It was hot over there, too—probably at least ten or fifteen degrees warmer than out in the hall." Okay, so maybe that estimate was a slight exaggeration, but it wasn't like I'd been able to take any readings with the dead thermometer. I pulled it out and turned it on; unlike the EMF reader, it still wasn't working.

Then I checked the photos. At least this time the images were actually there. I opened each JPEG on my laptop, blowing up the photos so they took up the entire screen. One by one, we inspected them for signs of anything paranormal. Each showed several orbs, little glowing balls of light that were common in photos containing supernatural activity. One of the last shots—one I'd taken of the shower alcove—showed a veil of bright white mist settled over the stalls.

"What the hell is that?" Tim said.

"I think it's ecto-mist," I said, although I'd never seen a really good example before and wasn't exactly sure what it was. "And see? It's only in the showers. It doesn't show up in any of the other pictures." I pointed to the screen. "That's what I sense when I'm in the locker room. That misty stuff gets around me and starts strangling me. I can feel it."

I'd also managed to get a single sound file before the digital recorder had gone dead. Using a program I'd downloaded from a ghost-hunting website, I manipulated the MP3 file, cleaning it up and eliminating as much of the ambient static as possible. I fiddled with the software's settings, then let the recording play on a loop.

"Did you hear that?" Tim asked, after we'd listened several times.

I shook my head; I didn't hear a thing.

"It starts around the seven-second mark." He turned up the volume on my laptop.

Now I could hear something if I really concentrated. It sounded like a whisper, gruff and garbled and almost inaudible. It hissed through the speakers, the undertone of a threat. It creeped me out, but I wasn't sure if the sound itself was responsible for the way my heart rate suddenly rabbited, or if I was reacting to what seemed to be its very eerie source. Was that the thing in the locker room talking?

What was it telling me?

"Let me try something," I said, plugging a pair of headphones into the laptop and listening through those. Eliminating the hiss of the speakers made the sound clearer and louder, and now I thought I could make out some distinct words.

"You . . ." the thing whispered. "You know . . ."

I held my breath, allowing the sound to loop over and over.

"You know . . . You can. No . . . Don't. She . . ." The voice paused, then hissed something else that I couldn't make out at first. It sounded like the name of a street, which made no sense. First Street? I didn't think Palmetto Crossing even had a First Street.

Then I began to hear the other sounds. The wails. Garbled, choking howls. Even quieter than the whisper, they cried in the background, a thousand miseries.

I yanked the headphones out of my ears and threw them onto the keyboard. "That's enough."

Then Tim took a listen. "'You can? No, don't?'" he repeated after a minute. "What's that mean?"

"I don't know. I couldn't make out all of it." I also couldn't stop shaking. "Can you hear the wailing in the background?"

He listened a little longer. "I hear . . . something, I guess. But what does it think you can do?"

I totally didn't want my mind to go there, but I couldn't help thinking about Tim's theory—that secret rituals were being held in the shower alcove, and that Coach Frucile was somehow involved.

"Maybe I'm next."

"Next for what?"

"It was your idea in the first place. Maybe this thing wants me as the next sacrifice."

For a long moment, we just stared at each other. I knew it was a ridiculous theory, but sometimes the what-ifs echo a lot louder in your mind than common sense.

"We can call the cops," Tim said finally.

"And tell them what? The police won't do anything based on some weird EMF readings and a tip from a couple of high school students."

"If something as illegal as human sacrifice is going on—"

"Okay. Enough." We were totally getting carried away. "We're just being stupid. My gym coach is not slicing and dicing students in the shower alcove after hours. It's just not happening, okay? Look, it's already mid-October. I'll keep wearing my gym clothes to school and changing in the bathroom until the semester ends, and then I'll never go near the locker room again. Problem solved. Whatever's in there can stay in there and fester; I don't care."

"Are you sure?"

"Yeah." I didn't know what else he expected me to do—pull a Ghostbusters jumpsuit out of my closet and strap some lights and sirens on Dad's hearse, maybe? I did wish I had someone I could talk to about it, but I didn't, and that was that. "It's fine. Let's just drop it." To punctuate my ruling, I reached over and deleted the sound file. "We're just hearing weird things in the static. So let's talk about something else."

Tim looked uncertain, but he did let it go. "Well . . . We could talk about Halloween, I guess."

"What about Halloween?" It was still two weeks away, and I hadn't even thought about it yet. Between getting settled with Dad and starting school and finding Mom's stuff and investigating the locker-room entity, my mind had been on other stuff.

Tim continued. "It's just that some of us were talking about going over to that cemetery on Longview, and, you know, hanging out, and Isobel was wondering if maybe you'd come, too." He spoke in such a practiced, nonchalant way that I knew he'd been dying to bring up the subject.

Hanging out in a cemetery on Halloween. It's sad when you have to try that hard to be a little spooky. Besides, the Longview Road Cemetery was hardly scary. It didn't even have interesting headstones; it was just row upon row of modern marble plaques set into the ground. I looked skeptically at Tim.

"Isobel was hoping we could, you know . . ."

"Spit it out, Timmy."

He glared at me a little, but at least it stopped his stuttering. I loved calling him Timmy when he annoyed me, and when he managed to annoy me, it usually had something to do with the goths. Aside from the few times I'd passed them in the hall, I'd been avoiding Tim's friends. Isobel just had too much of an attitude. Like I said, when you have to try that hard to be spooky . . .

"Isobel wants to have a séance in the cemetery," he said. "She wants you to lead it."

"No way, Tim!" Ugh, hadn't he been paying any attention at all when we read about the Ramsay Court investigation? "This is exactly the kind of stupid crap that causes issues like the ones in the Ramsay Court house. Idiots fooling around with things they don't understand."

"But you're not an idiot, and you do understand this stuff. You could keep it from getting dangerous."

"I barely understand any of it. I don't know anything about séances."

"You wouldn't need to. Just make them *think* you're doing one. We're all going either way, and . . . I'm kind of scared of what might happen if Isobel tries to lead the séance herself. I told her I'd ask you. Actually, I kind of told her I'd already asked you, and you said yes, so . . ." He gave me his best puppy-dog eyes; his smudged eyeliner made him look even more woeful.

Defeated, I gave him a look of doom. "Fine. Okay. I'll do it. But if they start doing stupid crap like trying to invoke demons or anything, I'm out of there."

I wondered briefly how it would look for Dad's business if his daughter got caught trespassing in a cemetery on Halloween night, but it didn't matter. After all, I didn't intend to get caught.

And I'd have to not get caught twice, since I intended to drop by the cemetery the night before Halloween to do a little negotiating with the locals.

After Tim left, I sat staring at my laptop for a long time. I thought about the thing in the locker room, and how Mom might've handled it.

Mom would never just throw out evidence. She would analyze it and catalog it. If it turned out to be false proof, she would note that as well, but she wouldn't just disregard it.

I dragged the sound file out of the recycling bin on my desktop and dropped it and the JPEGs into a folder I named *Locker-Room Investigation.* Then I wrote up a brief account of the investigation and saved that in the same folder. At least I thought I could rule out an actual hell gate, since I'd gotten that EVP. But if this was something else . . . what was it?

I really needed someone to talk to. Not just about the locker room. About everything.

I considered e-mailing the team that had done the Ramsay Court investigation, but their website made it pretty clear that they didn't have time for questions from amateur investigators.

That left me with just one other option—Sabrina Brightstar. I needed *someone* to guide me a little. Every time I thought about that hissing whisper in the recording, I felt more and more like I was in over my head.

Mom's address book didn't list a phone number or an e-mail address for Sabrina, but it did give me her real name—Mildred Schwartz—and a mailing address in Orlando. Snail mail it was, then. I wrote her a letter explaining who I was and that I was trying to find some information about my mother. I'd have to mail it closer to school, though; I couldn't leave the letter in our own street-side mailbox and risk Dad finding it. He'd freak if he knew who I was trying to contact.

I'd first met Sabrina and the team's fourth member, Bryan Chambers, at one of Mom and Dad's team dinner parties. (Bryan was notorious for freaking out halfway through investigations and hiding in the car—I knew he wouldn't be any help, so I hadn't even bothered trying to find him.) I remembered Sabrina as an older woman with short, frizzy gray hair and big, square-shaped eyeglasses. Her face was thin and creased, and she wore blue eye shadow all the way up to her brows. She wore tunics over flowing skirts and ridiculous amounts of clanky jewelry. She claimed to be psychic, drank a lot of wine, talked too loudly, smoked in the bathroom, and insulted my father's aura. She'd kind of scared me.

I remembered asking Mom about Sabrina once after one of those dinner parties.

"Why does she lie so much?" I'd asked Mom. I could tell Sabrina made a lot of stuff up. She embellished every story she told, trying to make herself sound like the awesomest person in the room.

"She doesn't lie, sweetie," Mom said. "At least, she doesn't mean to." She lifted me onto the counter and leaned over so we were eye to eye. "Some people really want to be special, Violet, like you and I are special. Sabrina's like that.

She has her own abilities, but that's not enough for her. She wants to be more like us, so she pretends sometimes. It's not okay to make things up, but sometimes if you understand why someone's doing it, you can cut them a little slack."

Mom was nice like that. She'd looked for the good in everyone. I wasn't nearly so forgiving.

CHAPTER EIGHT
séances and shiny things

While I waited to hear back from Sabrina, I stayed far away from the locker room and made myself concentrate on other things, like this faux séance I'd been talked into doing.

I'd need some supplies.

My first stop was Lovely Lily's, this store in the mall that sells supercheap, trendy costume jewelry and does ear piercing in the front window, as if watching people get holes punched in their lobes is some kind of free entertainment. In the clearance bin I found a couple of sparkly necklaces made from iridescent beads and bright silver-tone chain. They were hideous, but they'd do the trick.

(I also bought this awesome pair of glow-in-the-dark skull earrings from the shop's Halloween display, but those were just for me.)

After that, I checked out the sale racks at Striped

Skull, a dark, loud store that caters to the kind of goths and punks who hang out at suburban shopping malls. Okay, so I don't like to admit it, but I kind of love Striped Skull, even if I hate being associated with most of its clientele. At least now I had an excuse to do a little browsing—after all, if I was going to associate with the goths, I had to look the part. I ended up with some purple-and-black-striped tights, and a black lace shirt that looked like spiderwebs. The store also had an impressive display of heavy black boots, but they were all way out of my price range. I'd have to remember them for my Christmas list.

The night before Halloween, I put the beaded necklaces in my pocket and went downstairs to where Dad was about to embalm an old guy named Fred Whyte. While riding his three-wheeled bike to the supermarket, Fred had had an unfortunate encounter with a drunk driver in a pickup truck. Fred's face needed a lot of rebuilding and a heck of a lot of death spackle.

"I don't know why people insist on an open casket in situations like this," Dad said when I peeked in and asked how he was doing.

"Because at heart, people are stupid and morbid?" I suggested. "I just wanted to let you know I'm going for a walk."

Dad frowned. "It's almost nine o'clock."

"I know. I won't be long. Coach Frucile gave us these fitness journals," I lied, "and we're supposed to write down what kind of exercise we get every day. I need something to write for today."

"You could make something up," Dad said.

I pretended to be shocked and scandalized. "Surely you're not suggesting I cheat, Dad. High school gym is sooooo valuable and important. I have this incredible opportunity to challenge myself, and I refuse to squander it like that." I grinned. "I'll be back in less than an hour, I promise. And I have my phone. I'll be fine."

As usual, the Longview Road Cemetery had at least a dozen ghosts wandering around. Cemeteries tend to collect the spirits of the people who've been buried there. Most of them are waiting for something, usually for a spouse or family member to kick the bucket and join them. I mean, they're ghosts. It's not like they have anything better to do.

It's not as miserable as it sounds, though. There are always a bunch of them around, so there's always someone to talk to. They form friendships. They host parties. They mingle. They're very social.

It's a little weird.

The Longview Road Cemetery didn't have a dramatic wrought-iron gate, or even a decorative fence; it didn't get locked up at night. As far as cemeteries went, it was pretty lame and full of old people, just like the rest of Florida. I wandered in among the ghosts, ignoring a few comments I got along the way about whether I should be home in bed at this late hour. Thankfully, they all stopped talking when I held up the necklaces.

If there's one thing I've noticed over and over, it's that a lot of ghosts really, *really* like shiny things. I don't know why, but they do. The sparkling necklaces immediately caught the attention of two older ladies, who drifted over together and looked at me hopefully.

The shorter of the two ladies reached up and ran a ghostly finger over the beads; the necklace she touched shivered in my hand. "Pretty," she said.

"Aren't they?" I asked. "Ladies, I've got a necklace for each of you if you'll do me a favor tomorrow night."

The taller ghost clapped her wrinkled hands. "Ooh, this is fun! I can't remember the last time one of you live bodies could see us. Irma's a newbie, but I've been here for more than ten years. I'm waiting for my husband to join me. Don't know what's taking so damn long."

"That isn't nice, Delores," Irma fussed, still staring with fascination at the necklaces.

"Hrmph. He was slow as molasses when I was alive. Don't know why I expected that to change. Maybe I should go haunt him. That'll teach him."

"Delores. Really."

Delores ignored Irma and kept talking to me, apparently delighted to gossip with a living person. "He never listened to me when I was alive, either, the old grump. But here I am, his patient and loving wife, waiting for him. He'd better make sure he's buried next to me when the time comes, or I'll really let him have it. He used to say he wanted to be buried next to his mother in that cemetery across town. Can you believe that?"

Irma tsked at Delores, then addressed me. "What's your name, dear?"

"Violet," I said.

"What a lovely name. I had a cat named Violet once. Now, what sort of favor do you need?"

Quickly, I explained about Isobel and the goths and the séance situation.

"Oh, no." Delores shook her head. "You don't want to do that. Séances bring in all kinds of riffraff. We don't want that sort of thing in our neighborhood."

"That's exactly why I don't do séances," I agreed. "But these, um, friends of mine are expecting something spooky, so I was hoping you two could help." I told them my ideas, which they met with conspiratorial giggles. "So do we have a deal? If you help me out tomorrow, these necklaces are yours."

Both nodded. The movement made Irma's wispy white hair bounce a little before settling back over her forehead in a way that seemed familiar. She reminded me of someone I knew, but I couldn't think of who.

"This is going to be fun!" she said. "I think I'll quite enjoy scaring a couple of children. Kids today drive me crazy, what with their loud music and their ridiculous outfits and their horrible attitudes. Oh!" She gave me a sweet, grandmotherly smile. "Except for you, dear. You're a nice girl."

"Such a nice girl," Delores echoed. "What was your name again?"

"Violet."

Sigh. Old people. Death doesn't do a thing for their mental abilities. I just hoped they'd remember our deal.

CHAPTER NINE
night of the gothlings

Halloween worried Dad. Funeral homes were prime targets for vandalism, so he locked the hearse in the garage and set up a chair in the front driveway, where he could see everyone who passed. And since the funeral home was in a largely residential neighborhood, he kept a bowl of candy with him for any trick-or-treaters who wandered by. Most of them were too chicken to beg for handouts, though. Sheesh. Like a guy in jeans and a *Doctor Who* T-shirt is so scary, even if he does spend his days with dead bodies.

I wasn't meeting the goths until 11:00, so I brought out another chair and sat with Dad for a while. It was warm and humid, and the mosquitoes were out and buzzing, but at least the breeze had picked up after the sun went down.

Dad finally gave up around 9:30. Towns like Palmetto Crossing close down early, even on special nights like

Halloween; the trick-or-treaters had all disappeared about an hour earlier, and we hadn't even seen a car pass by in almost ten minutes.

"Night, Dad," I said as he headed inside. "I might stay out a little longer."

What? It wasn't technically a lie. I *was* planning to stay out, just not in our driveway. I knew it was kind of deceitful, but there was no way he would have let me go to the cemetery late at night if he knew my true plans.

"Okay. Let me know if you hear anything outside," he said. "You know I won't hear it." Dad's a notoriously sound sleeper, a fact that would make it a lot easier to sneak out in time to meet the goths.

I waited about ten minutes, then tiptoed inside to change into my spiderweb shirt, short black skirt, striped tights, and purple Chucks. I left my hair loose, letting it fall dark and straight over my shoulders and back, and carefully lined my eyes with black kohl. I had painted my nails black after school that day in preparation for the night's festivities, and with the addition of the skull earrings from Lovely Lily's, I thought I looked just spooky enough. I even kind of liked the look—not that I ever would've admitted it to Tim.

After filling my messenger bag with the necklaces and other supplies, I crept out into the hallway. I could hear Dad snoring already; getting out of the house without waking him up proved to be no problem.

I got to the cemetery a few minutes early. Longview Road was only three blocks away, and the streets between had been utterly deserted.

Amid the usual wandering spirits, I spotted Tim waiting for me in a long-sleeved black shirt and big black pants with lots of buckles and zippers on them.

"Thanks for coming," he said, looking relieved.

I wondered if he'd thought I'd go back on my word.

"Here." He dropped something light and metallic—a length of chain—into my hand. "This is for you. To say thank you. I got it for you. I mean, I made it. It's probably stupid."

I held it up. It was a bracelet, made from a series of little purple and black jump rings linked in a pattern. "It's not stupid. It's really pretty."

"Really? It's chain mail. I found this website that explained how to make it, and it's kind of, like, you know, my hobby or something, but I wasn't sure . . ." He shifted awkwardly from one foot to the other. "The purple links are metal, but the black ones are rubber, so the bracelet stretches."

"I love it." I slipped it on my left wrist, where it peeked out from under the sleeve of my spiderweb shirt. "Thank you."

I wanted to know more about his hobby, but we were interrupted by the sound of footsteps behind us. I turned and saw five mostly dark shapes with pale faces—Isobel and four of her gothlings—walking toward us in an almost solid black wave of lace and velvet and shiny PVC vinyl. They stomped over graves and flat headstones in their big black boots. Several of the elderly ghosts shot them dirty glances.

Isobel smiled, sort of, when she reached us. The corners of her red-black lips quirked upward. She put on such an act of constant serious, gothic misery that I thought a full smile might've shattered her face.

Her posse was not quite so disciplined, though. Two of them grinned openly, one jumped around and clapped his hands, and the last looked vaguely queasy, like she wanted to go home.

"You came to our All Hallow's Eve celebration," Isobel said to me. Her smile was gone but her tone remained as affected as the rest of her. "I am delighted." I was glad she told me, since I never would've described her detached stare and ultra-arched eyebrows as anything close to "delighted."

"Thanks for inviting me," I said. "Tim convinced me to come, though."

Tim gave me a quick smile.

Isobel nodded briefly in his direction. "You did well."

Tim looked so full of bliss that I thought he might

pass out from just that much attention from her. Good lord. Isobel really was Queen of the Goths, wasn't she?

"We understand you are prepared to help us communicate with the dark spirits," Isobel said. She touched a hand to her throat, as if she were subtly trying to bring attention to her black lace gloves or the red stone ring on her middle finger. I recognized both from my last trip to Striped Skull.

Several nearby ghosts rolled their eyes or shook their translucent fists in Isobel's direction. I glanced around at them, hoping to see Irma and Delores.

"Communicating with dark spirits can be extremely dangerous," I said. "However—"

"I told you!" the worried girl said to Isobel. "This is totally not cool. I don't want to end up, like, possessed or something."

"Like you should be so lucky," Isobel growled at her.

"I'm serious! We could unleash some bad stuff. Haven't you seen any of those *Exorcist* movies?" Worried Girl said.

Isobel shot her a withering look. "Shut up, Charlene."

"Nightshade," Worried Girl corrected with a pout. "How come you won't call me by my chosen name?"

"I'll call you by your chosen name when you choose one that's not such a stupid cliché," Isobel said.

Accusing someone else in her goth posse of being a cliché seemed awfully hypocritical of her. I mean, pale makeup? Lots of eyeliner? Dyed black hair? Hello?

Charlene made a vile face behind her leader's back. I had a feeling she was eagerly wishing possession and anything else the dark spirits could cook up on Isobel.

"Please continue," Isobel said to me.

"I'm ready to guide us through a séance," I said, gagging inwardly at the thought. "I can't promise you any dark spirits, but if we're lucky, we should be able to communicate with someone."

Isobel nodded. "That will do nicely."

Since I had no intention of holding anything resembling a real séance, I was pulling fake details out of my butt. I ordered the goths to sit in a circle on an empty gravesite. As they watched in fascination, I pulled out a sandwich bag full of dirt.

"This soil was stolen from a fresh grave by my great-grandmother in 1907," I said importantly. Really, I'd dug it out of one of the decorative planters in front of the funeral home that afternoon. "It has been blessed by, um, a dark coven. It will aid us in the invocation of the dead, and protect us from unnecessary harm." I sprinkled some of the dirt around the outside of the circle of goths, all while somehow keeping a straight face.

Nearby, the ghost of an old man in plaid golf shorts and a polo watched me, shaking his head in disgust. Irma—she'd remembered our deal after all, thank goodness—appeared by his side and whispered in his ear. As she explained what I was really up to, his scowl disappeared and he chuckled and nodded. Irma winked at me. A moment later I spotted Delores standing off to one side, too.

"Next, the flame of the living," I continued. A bunch of candles would've done a lot for the spooky atmosphere, but I wasn't about to set up a funerary fire hazard for the sake of Tim's reputation, so I'd settled for a single black candle. I lit it and carried it around the circle, waving it in the air. "Fire represents life. It moves and it consumes. Its warmth will attract the spirits to us."

The old man in the golf shorts cackled and drifted forward several feet, waving his arms and pretending to be drawn toward the flame. I very nearly lost it, but I set my jaw and kept my composure, carefully placing the candle in the center of the circle and pressing it into the earth to make sure it would stay upright.

Finally I produced two glass spheres, one opaque black, one clear. They'd been in Mom's boxes; once upon a time they'd been displayed on a pair of stands on one of her bookshelves. They weren't powerful or charged with energy or anything, she'd just thought they were pretty.

But the goths didn't know that.

I held up the spheres in front of them. "Crystal balls," I said. "This is how the spirits will communicate with us. This one means yes"—I indicated the clear ball—"and this one means no." I waved the black ball around for emphasis. Stepping into the circle again, I placed both balls on the gravesite, one on either side of the candle. Then I took my spot in the circle and made everyone link hands.

"Oh, spirits!" I said, pretending to concentrate really hard. "We humbly request your presence in our circle of invocation on this All Hallow's Eve." The wind picked up around us, which was a nice touch, even though it was a total coincidence. "If you are here with us, please make yourselves known."

Giggling, Irma floated into the circle and tried to nudge the clear ball with her foot. Some ghosts have trouble connecting with physical objects, so it took her a few tries. After a moment, though, the ball shivered in the dirt. Irma tried once more, and this time the ball rolled an inch or two. Isobel stared with wide eyes and made that twitchy smile again; Charlene appeared about to cry. The other goths looked like they might go either way.

"Thank you, O spirit!" I said. "May we ask you some questions?"

The clear ball bumped forward again. It rolled in the direction of Charlene, who scooted back a few inches.

"Got any questions?" I asked the goths.

"What's his name?" asked the guy who had jumped and clapped.

"It has to be a yes or no question, stupid!" Isobel snarled.

The guy looked embarrassed.

"There are ways to ask other kinds of questions," I said, happy to contradict Isobel. "Spirit! May we try to decipher your name?"

The clear ball moved.

"Does it begin with an *A*?"

The black ball moved.

"A *B*?"

The black ball rocked forward again. I knew Irma was making up a fake ghostly identity; I just hoped she hadn't decided to name him Zachary.

"A *C*?"

The clear ball moved.

"In life, O spirit, were you a man?" I asked, to cut down the list of possibilities.

The clear ball moved. *Yes.*

We went around the circle, suggesting male names that started with C, until Irma settled on "Charlie."

"Charlie," I said, "are you buried in this very cemetery?"

Yes.

"Ooh, ooh," the jumping guy said. "Did you die violently?"

Yes.

Except for Charlene, the goths looked impressed.

"Were you murdered?" the same guy asked. He was really getting the hang of this.

No.

"Was it an accident?"

Yes.

"That's not scary enough!" Delores hissed at Irma. Irma immediately rethought her answer and kicked the black ball instead.

The jumping goth hesitated. "Were you executed?"

Yes. Oh, Irma was having some fun with this.

"Did you murder someone?" I asked.

Yes.

"More than one person?"

Yes.

"More than five?"

Yes.

Well, this could go on all night. "I've heard this legend," I fibbed to the goths. "There's supposed to be a serial killer buried in this very cemetery. Even in death, he still seeks new victims. They say you'll know he's nearby when you hear his footsteps. Yes, that's right," I emphasized for the benefit of my life-impaired accomplices and hoped they'd get the hint. "His loud footsteps. Charlie! Is this why you are still here with us, spirit? Are you doomed to walk the earth in penance for your terrible crimes?"

Yes.

Charlene stood up. "Screw this," she said, her voice wavering. She stalked off.

I decided to work her exit into the show. Trying to look panicked, I said, "Our circle of protection has been broken. We must quickly tie Charlie back to his grave before he is loosed upon us!"

Everyone looked appropriately nervous, even Isobel. Heck, even Tim looked genuinely anxious, and he knew none of this was real.

"Repeat this with me," I said. "Your time on earth is done; you must leave us alone." I was pretty proud of myself for coming up with a rhyme—okay, a slant rhyme—on the spur of the moment like that.

Holding hands, the group repeated the line over and over. Now Irma really started getting into her role. Her face twisted in concentration, she reached down and scooped up the black ball. To everyone but me, it looked like the "no" ball had begun to levitate. Irma carried it out of the circle and paraded around with it.

The goths all looked as if they suddenly thought Charlene had been wise to run.

Then the footsteps started nearby—finally. They were heavy and solid; I could hear the grass crunch. Even though I knew it was just Delores stomping around as loudly as she could, the effect was enough to give even me a chill.

Isobel screamed. Yanking her hand away, she scrambled to her feet and took off, running as fast as her industrial platform boots could carry her. The other goths, no longer worried about looking stupid in front of their leader, followed. Tim and I stood up and watched them retreat. Irma and Delores drifted nearby, both doubled over with laughter. Irma let the black ball fall onto the grass.

"That was really awesome," Tim said. "How'd you do the footsteps thing?"

I glanced around, pretending to be afraid again. "I didn't plan that part."

"What?!"

"I'm kidding! Don't pass out or anything."

He toed the ground. "I knew you were kidding."

"Sure you did." I retrieved the black ball from where Irma had dropped it, then blew out the candle and packed everything up.

"Want me to walk you home?" Tim asked.

"Sure, thanks. There's just one more thing I have to do first. Well, two more things." I took out the necklaces and approached Irma and Delores. "Wonderful job, ladies. Thank you. Where do you want these?"

"Oh, I'm right over there," Irma said, motioning for me to follow. "And Delores is two rows closer. We'll show you."

As Irma led the way, Delores floated along beside me.

"So pretty," she said, her eyes fixed on the necklaces,

which glimmered in the moonlight. "My Henry never gave me anything this nice in forty years of marriage."

"Your husband's name is Henry?" I asked, thinking of the dead janitor who was now spooking around school, hassling me every time I tracked in mud or left fingerprints on a clean window. It couldn't be the same Henry. Could it?

"Yes," Delores said, still paying more attention to the necklaces than me.

"Henry Boyd?"

That caught her attention. "That's him. How did you know?"

"Delores, I'm so sorry to have to tell you this, but your husband passed away about two months ago. My dad's funeral home handled his arrangements."

I thought the news might upset her, but instead she just scowled. "That can't be right. I've been waiting for him for years. If he went and had himself buried next to his mother . . . Did this Henry need a haircut?"

"In the worst way," I said, picturing Henry's thinning curls.

"Thank you for telling me, dear. As soon as I find that deceitful old goat, I'll give him what for."

"He's back at Palmetto High School," I said. "You should be able to find him there." I didn't have even a twinge of guilt about tattling on Henry.

I draped Delores's necklace over the plaque that served as her headstone. "Are you sure I can't leave them somewhere safer?" I asked as I followed Irma to her grave. "The maintenance people will find them, or visitors will take them." It was a shame the ladies couldn't just wear their new treasures, but it wouldn't be wise to have a couple of necklaces levitating around the cemetery.

"Oh, we know," Irma said. "But at least we can enjoy them for a little while first. I do so love shiny things."

She pointed out her plot; when I went to put the necklace down, I saw her full name and gasped. "Irma Morris? Wait, you're Mrs. Morris, aren't you?" I knew Irma had looked familiar! The last time I'd seen her, she was silent and still, covered in death spackle and laid out for her viewing.

"Yes, dear. That's me." Irma looked a little confused.

"My dad owns Addison Funeral Services," I explained. "I did your de—I mean, I did your makeup."

"How nice of you, Violet." Irma smiled and patted my arm, a gesture that felt like nothing more than a draft of cool air. "I took a peek before they put me in the ground, you know. I looked very pretty."

"You're such a nice girl," Delores added. "Come visit us again sometime. I want you to meet my son."

Irma clucked her tongue. "Delores, your son is thirty-eight years old and has a potbelly. Violet can do better."

Delores gave her friend an icy glare.

Before an old-ghost-lady catfight could break out, I said good-bye to Irma and Delores and turned back to Tim. He was staring nervously at the necklace on Irma's headstone. Irma was nudging it with her toe, making it move back and forth so that it twinkled in the moonlight.

"Oh, come on," I said as I hoisted the messenger bag over my shoulder and started for home. "You can't tell me you're not getting at least a little used to this stuff by now."

Tim still seemed a little jumpy. "That wasn't . . . I mean, that wasn't really Charlie back there, was it?"

"There is no Charlie."

"Are you sure?"

"You really think a serial killer named Charlie would be interested in cheap costume jewelry from the mall?"

"Well, you never know."

I gave him an exasperated glance. I guess séances—even the fake kind—aren't for everyone.

CHAPTER TEN
the black rose

After Halloween night, I was unwilling royalty among the goths. I guess my faux séance had truly impressed them, or else they were terrified I'd sic the ghost of Charlie the serial killer on them if they didn't kiss my butt a little. Either way, they did their best to welcome me into their ranks no matter how hard I resisted, and Isobel tolerated Tim because he was my friend. I put up with all of it because Tim was in black-eyeliner heaven.

(Okay, and because it's nice to be adored instead of mocked, no matter who's doing the adoring.)

The following Monday, Tim and I were on the second floor of the east building, heading to the library for lunch. As we passed a door that was slightly ajar, we heard a quick, conspiratorial hiss. It was Derek, the jumping goth, peeking out from behind the door.

"Come here."

The door led to one of the emergency stairwells that allowed access to the roof, which was why students weren't normally allowed to use it. The fire code prohibited the school from keeping the stairwells locked, but the doors were equipped with alarms to keep anyone from sneaking in. Except for this door, apparently. When I asked Derek, he explained that the stairwell's alarm had been broken since last spring.

"The administration's too busy with important crap like dress code violations and football games to notice," he said, smirking.

The trapdoor to the roof was already open; we followed Derek up the ladder and found the rest of the goths already there, shading themselves from the sun with umbrellas and passing around a bottle of what had to be industrial-strength sunscreen.

We sat down with them; they weren't my favorite people to spend a lunch period with, but the breeze felt so nice that I didn't care about the company. The first cold front of the fall had moved through over the weekend, and the weather was surprisingly cool—for Florida, at least—and pleasant. It did seem like an awfully sunny choice for a bunch of creatures of the night, but I guess the roof's isolation in an otherwise overcrowded school was worth a little sun exposure.

"You okay up here, Mister Half Vampire?" I asked Tim.

He put on his sunglasses and held up his hand, shielding part of his face. "I'll be fine."

"We spend lunch up here every day," Derek said, sitting beside us, "except when it looks like it might rain. Charlene's afraid of getting hit by lightning."

"Three thousand people die from lightning strikes every year in Florida," Charlene informed us as she rubbed sunscreen on the back of her neck.

"That sounds a little high," I said.

"Look it up," she huffed.

I shrugged. "Hey, the more people who get hit by lightning, the more business for my dad."

Charlene sneered, but the rest of the goths looked interested, as if they hoped for more funerary anecdotes. Then Isobel glanced over the edge of the building at the central courtyard below and made an offended *hmm* sound, and all attention returned to her.

"Behold, the void," she said flatly. "It assembles."

I followed her gaze. In the courtyard, a herd of jocks and cheerleaders gathered around one of the long planters that ran along either side of the sundial. A series of pizza boxes sat on the planter's ledge; the jocks were enthralled by the pizza, and the cheerleaders were enthralled by the jocks. I saw Cherry picking the pepperoni off her slice and feeding each piece to Jake Bartle by hand.

It was a school rule that everyone had to spend the lunch period in the cafeteria, (unless, of course, you found an unobtrusive place to hide). Like the dress code, that rule apparently didn't apply to the jocks or the cheerleaders. They'd never get in trouble for skipping lunch and hanging out in the courtyard, but we were risking detention or worse.

"How'd they get the pizza?" I asked.

"One of them probably left campus to get it," Derek said. "Or maybe they got it delivered right to the front office."

"And that's allowed?"

Isobel rolled her eyes. "For the void? Of course."

I had to admit, as far as nicknames went, "the void" was a pretty good fit.

"I'm surprised Dead Dirk's not following them around," I said, squinting. "Then again, it can be hard to see ghosts when the sun's this bright. It turns them kind of transparent."

I'd assumed Tim had told the goths all about the ghost in the art wing, but judging by Isobel's quick response, I was wrong.

"Dirk Reynolds?" she asked, uncharacteristically quietly. "He's still here? You can see him?" The usual affectation was temporarily gone from her voice.

"I've only seen him in one of the art rooms," I said, taking note of Isobel's sudden interest. I hadn't noticed before, but now I realized I'd never spotted Dirk around the jocks anywhere else at school. Only in drawing class.

"And he's there regularly?"

"Yeah. I see him a couple times a week."

"Will you do me a favor?" Beneath her frilly black parasol, Isobel tilted her head. "Ask Dirk about the black rose, and tell me what he says."

I was surprised by her request, but I nodded. "Sure. I can't promise anything, though. He doesn't like me."

As I thought about Isobel's cryptic question, I began to wonder if maybe there was a reason I'd only ever seen Dirk in the art room. A reason that had nothing to do with the jocks.

I didn't get to ask Tim about Isobel's request until we were on our way to drawing class, and he didn't have any idea what it was about.

"I can't imagine they would've been friends," I mused. "A star athlete and the queen of the goths?"

"Isobel was a freshman when Dirk was a junior," Tim said. "So I guess it could be possible. But can you imagine the two of them hanging out?"

"Nope. Maybe Dirk used to tease her or something. Maybe the black rose is some sort of code for something he did. She seemed interested in the fact that he's always in the art wing."

"Isobel's a great artist," Tim said. "Her stuff ends up in the state art fair every year. She has Advanced Portfolio first period—you can't get into that class without advance approval from the teacher. And you know that mural in the hall by the gym?"

"That ugly Trojan?"

"Yep. That one."

"It's all crooked and out of proportion."

"I know. She did that on purpose because she hates Palmetto so much. There was a contest last year to see who'd get to paint the mural. The winning design was guaranteed to be up for at least a year. So Isobel did this really great sketch—I mean, it was a Trojan with a sword and a football, so it was still stupid, but it looked professional. So she won, but when she painted the final mural, she pretended to have trouble with the proportions. She made all these, like, mistakes. On purpose. And it has to stay up because she won the contest. The art teachers all know what she did, but they won't say anything because they're all pissed that the sports programs get all the funding while the art programs keep getting cut. It was pretty brilliant."

"Wow." Clearly, I hadn't given Isobel enough credit. Her trick with the mural was pretty ballsy. I could definitely get behind someone who hated Palmetto as much as she did, even if she did seem a little too interested in one of its former star athletes.

Dirk was present during class that day, ghosting around near the portfolio racks. After twenty minutes of drawing a bowl of fruit with sepia-colored Conté sticks, I pretended I needed to check something in my portfolio and wandered over to the racks.

"Hey," I whispered when I was close to Dirk. "You know Isobel? Tall girl, black hair, queen of the goths?"

Dirk gave me a strange, wary look. "Yeah. But her hair was brown when I knew her."

Like I cared. "She wanted me to ask you about the black rose."

"What?" His eyes widened. "Tell her it's gone."

"What's that supposed to mean?"

"Figure it out," he said, and he vanished. Ghosts can be so damned cryptic.

It wasn't much of a message to relay, but I shared it with Isobel on the roof during lunch the next day. It seemed to upset her. "Tell him I won't accept that."

"I will, but it would help if I knew what we're talking about."

Isobel sighed and glanced at her fellow goths. Then she stood up and tilted her head, indicating that I should follow her to the opposite end of the roof. The others stared after us in awe, as though I'd been awarded a private audience with a celebrity.

"I can't talk about this in front of them," Isobel said when we were out of earshot. "I promised Dirk I'd never tell, but this has been bothering me since he . . . you know. Since he died." She looked troubled. "He's not here right now, is he?"

"I've never seen him anywhere but the art room. I'm starting to think he might be stuck there."

She nodded. "I think I might know why. See, everyone thinks Dirk was dating that Cherry skank his junior year. She spread that around after he died because it got her a lot of attention. But really, he couldn't stand her. And he was sort of involved with someone else." Her expression was uncomfortable and almost embarrassed. "Me."

I suppose I'd seen that coming, but hearing her admit it still surprised me a little.

"You? And part of the void?"

"He wasn't like the others," she said. "Not really. He did the football thing because he was good at it, but also, mostly, because his dad pushed him. His dad used to tell him he was stupid, and that football was the only way he'd get into college. Dirk wasn't stupid." Isobel's voice grew defensive. "I mean, he wasn't great at math and stuff, so his grades were crappy. But he didn't deserve to be put down like that by his own dad. He had so much going for him besides sports." She paused, as though she needed to collect her thoughts. "I first met him in the art wing, in room 314."

"That's where my drawing class is," I said.

She nodded. "Yeah, I figured it was the same room. This was back when I was a freshman. Mr. Connelly let me stay late one afternoon to finish a project. About twenty minutes after the last bell rang, Dirk came in and started setting up an easel across the room. He didn't say anything, just got a canvas and some acrylics and started painting. He was doing this abstract thing with reds and purples and oranges. It was anger and frustration in big, bold blocks of color. Every so often Mr. Connelly would go over and give him advice—not that he really needed it. The painting was amazing."

Isobel went on with her story. Mr. Connelly liked her work and wanted her to submit some pieces to the county's annual exhibit, so she started staying late every day to get them done. Sometimes Dirk was there, sometimes he wasn't. On the days he showed up, he usually painted; occasionally he sketched instead. He always worked in silence, until one day when he stepped back from his canvas and asked Isobel what she thought of his latest painting. After that, they started talking pretty regularly.

"Dirk had talent. He was the one who should've been submitting to exhibits and stuff," Isobel said, "but his dad wouldn't let him. The jerk said it was a waste of time that should've gone into more football practice instead." Since Dirk's dad wouldn't let him take art classes, Mr. Connelly let Dirk work in the art wing before or after school, depending on his football practice schedule, of course. Dirk's dad thought he was spending that time either out on the field or in the gym's weight room.

Because of all the pressure from his father, Dirk was almost ashamed of how much he enjoyed painting. He vented a lot to Isobel, and she vented back about how much she hated school. Their various miseries put them on a surprisingly compatible wavelength.

"It all had to be kind of secret because Dirk was terrified of his dad finding out. How stupid is that? A six-foot-four football player being scared of his worthless little jerk of a father who couldn't just accept his son for who he was." Dirk was so secretive about his art that his entire relationship with Isobel played out inside room 314. They never so much as got coffee or saw a movie together.

Despite that, I could tell from the pain in Isobel's voice just how serious their connection had been. She loved him; I could hear it in the way she still tried to protect him from his dad's judgment.

"The Black Rose was an oil painting Dirk had been working on. He said he was dedicating it to me. I didn't really have my look together back then, but I was already wearing a lot of black, and he knew I was thinking about dyeing my hair. The painting was gorgeous—it was this abstract, geometric rose done in black against a white background with all these sharp lines and jagged shapes. It kind of looked like stained glass without the color added in. I was going to keep harassing him until he agreed to put it in the county exhibition, but then he went to that stupid party and . . .

"What a dumbass thing to do." Her voice softened, and she stared into the distance. "Drinking that much and then thinking he could drive home. But that's how he acted around the other jocks. He turned into exactly what you'd expect, just another member of the void. I never even bothered trying to talk to him outside of the art room. But when he was painting, it was like he became a different person. I think that's the only time he was able to be himself. That's why I'm not surprised he's still hanging around in room 314. It's where he was happiest." She was blinking rapidly, and she smiled almost apologetically. "I shouldn't cry. I'll smudge my stupid mascara."

What she said also explained why Dirk had gotten mad when I'd ratted him out to the jocks. He was still trying to be one of them. He was afraid of being different.

After taking a few breaths and composing herself,

Isobel continued. "The painting was almost done when he died. The last time I saw him work on it was a few days before the accident, and it just needed the finishing touches. But I didn't know where he put it. I left the art room before he did that day, and I don't know if he left the painting there or took it with him. When he was working on a painting, he usually left the easel facing the corner by the supply closets so the paint could dry. Sometimes he left finished paintings in that space by Mr. Connelly's desk, between the wall and the file cabinet. I checked as soon as I could after I heard about the accident. The painting wasn't on an easel, so I figured it was dried, but it wasn't by the file cabinet, either, and Mr. Connelly didn't know where it was. So I thought, since you can still talk to Dirk . . ."

"You want the painting because it was supposed to be for you."

"No." She glanced down at her boots. "I want to submit it to this year's art show under his name. I think that would be allowed, as long as Mr. Connelly signs off on it. Dirk was so stubborn about keeping his art private, but he was really good. I want the world to see at least one of his pieces."

I shrugged. "Based on his reaction to your question, I'm not sure he'd want that."

"I don't care what he wants." She shook her head,

suddenly aggravated. "I'm so damned mad at him still. He had all that talent, and he wasted it. He practically wasted his whole life being a member of the void. Now he's gone, and his work deserves to be seen." She looked pleadingly at me. "Ask him again. Or let me talk to him. Can you do that? Like, repeat what he says to me? Since I can't hear him?"

That had always been my mom's thing—reconnecting ghosts to their living loved ones, letting them communicate, helping them move on. Mom's gift was more than just seeing spirits. She also wanted to help them. I wasn't like that. If there was anything I'd inherited from my dad, it was the belief that dead people—corpses, not ghosts— were easier to deal with than their living counterparts. I didn't want to deal with a bunch of personal drama.

Still, I found myself nodding. "We can try that. Let me talk to him again first, though."

Not that I had any idea what I was going to say.

CHAPTER ELEVEN
aura treatments and psychic echoes

I arrived home that afternoon to find Sabrina Brightstar's letter with a huge RETURN TO SENDER stamped on it. I was bummed but not surprised, since it wasn't like Mom had been around to update her address book. I'd just have to do a little more in-depth sleuthing.

A search of the Internet white pages for Sabrina Brightstar or Mildred Schwartz brought up nothing, but I struck some very tacky gold when I did a more general search. Sabrina Brightstar had her very own website. It was horrendous—not that I'm an expert in web design, but wow. Animated graphics, blinking neon text, and one of those annoying embedded MIDI files that starts playing blippy electronic music as soon as the site loads. (Sabrina's song of choice was an elevator-music version of "Every Little Thing She Does Is Magic" by The Police.) It was the kind of disaster someone with no taste and a copy of one of those web design books for dummies might've come up with circa 2003.

This Sabrina Brightstar—and really, how many could there be?—sold tarot card readings, astrological counseling sessions, and aura treatments (whatever those were) online. A quick scan of her "About Me" page revealed that, although she currently lived in Colorado, she'd spent a decade on the east coast of Florida. Yep, this had to be the same Sabrina. I shot her a quick e-mail, again explaining that I was looking for information about my mom and the Logan Street investigation. Her response showed up the following afternoon.

> Dear Violet:
> Of course I remember you, dear. I knew you would soon contact me. Your thoughts of me gave you away; I felt every one of them. I sensed you were curious about your mother as well.

I almost gave up on her right then. She "sensed" that I was curious? Wasn't that kind of obvious from the whole, what-can-you-tell-me-about-my-mother thing? This was worse than one of those cold readings the fake psychics do on talk shows. But I slogged on through, hoping to find a valuable detail or two.

Your mother was a wonderful woman and a dear friend, and it still pains me to remember what happened to her that awful night. I'm not sure how much you know about my abilities—

Shouldn't she have been able to sense that, too? I mean, I'm the last person to arbitrarily doubt someone else's abilities, but still. I couldn't help snickering.

—but I am a powerful psychic and empath, and I feel things far more keenly than most people. Your mother, Robin, always appreciated my gifts. She understood what it felt like to be different in such a way; I sense that you understand as well. I knew of your gift as soon as I met you, well before your mother told me about it.

You said you wanted to know more about what happened that night. The Logan Street property was so full of negative energies that I could barely set foot inside. However, your mother depended on my expertise, so I forced myself onward. That house, Violet, was unlike anything I'd ever experienced. The presence within was angry and terrifying, and it left its invisible mark throughout the structure. Have you heard of psychic echoes? Occurrences involving strong emotion can imprint the surrounding area with an "echo" of that emotion. The echo repeats itself over and over, caught in an unending loop. Those with gifts like mine can sense such echoes and understand the circumstances behind them. This is why your mother relied on me—she could sense and speak to spirits, but only I could interpret a location's echoes and determine the truth.

SPOOKYGIRL : paranormal investigator

I was overwhelmed by the echoes in the Logan
Street house. I'm not sure how much you know about how
Palmetto Paranormal operated, but in most cases, we did
a preliminary investigation during the day, then returned at
night, when supernatural elements are at their most active,
for a more in-depth investigation. During the preliminary of
Logan Street, I inferred a strong sense of violence and wrath
emanating from the property. So many bad things happened
there, and all the echoes centered upon James Riley, Jr.,
and his wife, Abigail. I felt such rage around them! It was
obvious to me that James Riley was, in life, an abusive
husband, exposing Abigail to the brunt of his terrible temper.
A whisper of infidelity wafted through the house—as I
studied the echo, I grew certain James suspected Abigail of
being unfaithful. Perhaps it was that lack of trust which led to
their downfall and maybe even their deaths.

Grasping the nuances of the situation was difficult.
There were too many echoes at that point, too many
remnants of rage and hatred and pain. Such things are not
always clear, even to me.

But that night . . . My dear, that night was horrible.
The house had no electricity and my flashlight stopped
working almost immediately. The darkness increased the
echoes tenfold, both in volume and in strength. Our fourth
member, Bryan, abandoned the investigation after only a few
minutes, but I did my best to persevere because I knew it
was important to Robin. After I'd gathered what information
I could, I went looking for your parents to tell them I was
finished and would wait outside. In a flash of lightning, I
spotted your mother at the top of the stairs with a dark,

threatening figure standing next to her. It reached out and shoved her, and she fell.

I may not be a young woman, and my eyesight is not what it used to be, but I know what I saw. I also know that the only people in that house were your mother, your father, and me. Who else could it have been?

I wish I had more insight for you, dear, but that is all I know.

Yours,

Sabrina Brightstar

A dark, threatening figure? Why was she so certain it was Dad? It could have been a weird shadow caused by the lightning. Heck, maybe it was the ghost of James Riley, Jr. Maybe he was such a strong spirit that even an airhead like Sabrina could catch a glimpse.

But if that were true . . . Could James Riley, Jr., have pushed my mother? How many times had Mom told me things like that couldn't happen, that the dead wouldn't, or couldn't, physically harm the living in such a direct way?

Still, I suddenly find myself doubting Mom. Maybe she'd just wanted to believe what she'd told me, or maybe she'd been too busy looking for the good in everyone, living or dead, to see that some people just don't have any good in them at all.

And why *couldn't* a ghost hurt a living person? Even harmless Irma Morris from the cemetery could heft around a few glass balls. If she'd wanted to hurt any of us, she could have lobbed them at our heads. And look at Buster—if he was able to turn an entire room of furniture upside down, surely he could throw stuff hard enough to cause an injury.

Or shove someone down a flight of stairs.

At least I knew ghosts like Buster and Irma wouldn't do things like that, but I had no reason to trust James Riley, Jr.

An idea began to spin in the back of my mind. It was ridiculous, and probably dangerous, and I knew I should ignore it, but . . . I wasn't going to be able to finish the Logan Street investigation with only secondhand information from an incompetent psychic. I needed a more direct approach.

What if I went to the Logan Street property and did some investigating of my own? I was certain Dad hadn't pushed Mom, but if I could go to that house, hopefully confront a ghost or two, and find out what really happened, maybe I'd be able to complete the file with a concrete statement that would put a lot more than the unfinished investigation to rest.

Pulling this off wouldn't be easy. I'd need a plan—a better plan than I'd come up with for investigating the locker room. But I felt more and more determined to finish

Mom's final investigation file, and this seemed like the only way to do it.

Feeling excited but still annoyed at Sabrina, I printed her e-mail and added it to the Logan Street folder. It was important to be as complete and comprehensive as possible with these things. If I was going to do this, I was going to do it Mom's way through and through. And that meant compiling any and all information.

Unfortunately, to be really complete, the Logan Street folder also needed another person's account—my dad's— and I knew I wasn't going to have much luck getting that. The more I thought about it, though, the more it seemed like the folder needed a fourth account, too. Mine. I mean, I wasn't there that night, but I was certainly a part of the bigger picture.

That's when I remembered Ms. Geller's midterm assignment: the descriptive essay about my most vivid childhood memory. Denying it any longer was stupid—I knew exactly what I had to write about, exactly which memory I had to face.

Violet Addison
November 14
English 2 Honors
Most Vivid Childhood Memory

Black Tourmaline

When I think about the night my mom died, the first thing I remember is black tourmaline. Mom always carried a small piece of tourmaline—inky black and cold and tumbled smooth—among her lucky charms. She was a paranormal investigator, and she believed tourmaline offered protection against negative energy. I just thought it was a pretty rock, so I was always taking it out of her messenger bag and trying to keep it for myself. It made me feel like I always had a piece of her nearby.

That evening, while my mom was getting ready for an investigation, I stole the tourmaline out of her bag. I thought I could keep it for the night, then put it back in the morning without her ever knowing. Then she and Dad left for the Logan Street house.

I never saw her again.

Everything else from that night is a blurred string of connected memories. I went to bed at 9:30 as usual, and left the tourmaline on my nightstand, where it would be safe. Then the phone rang, waking me up just enough to hear my babysitter, Rachel, answer. I must have fallen back to sleep quickly, though, because I didn't hear her end of the conversation. When I woke up again, my bedside lamp was on and Aunt Thelma was in my room. She told me to get dressed, then got my purple suitcase out of the closet and began packing some of my clothes.

I was groggy and confused. I told her it was too early to get up, and I asked where my mom and dad were.

"Your dad's at my house in Lakewood," she said. "That's where we're going now."

That confused me even more. "But where's Mom? Is she there, too?"

"You just wait and talk to your dad, okay?" Aunt Thelma's eyes were red and watery. "I can't do that part for him."

I didn't know what she meant, and I shoved away the clothes she tried to hand me. She was giving me my Saturday jeans to wear, the ones with the holes in the knees. It was a school day; Mom wouldn't let me wear those jeans to school. Aunt Thelma said I wouldn't have to go to school that day.

That was when I realized something had to be wrong. I was scared. I didn't want to go to Aunt Thelma's house. I wanted my mom and dad.

When we got to Aunt Thelma's house, Dad was waiting in the living room. His face was white and his eyes were puffy, and his expression made him look like a balloon someone had let all the air out of. I'd never seen him look like that before. Not my dad, who forgot the punch lines when he told jokes, and who made us sit through bad science fiction movies on cable, and who laughed more than anyone else I knew, except maybe my mom.

He held his arms out, and I ran to him and hugged him as hard as I could.

"Thank you, kiddo." He hugged me back just as tightly. "I really, really needed that."

Aunt Thelma kept offering to get us tea or coffee or milk, I guess because she didn't know what else to do.

I don't remember exactly how he told me, the words he chose. There was a lot of crying. Mom had fallen down a flight of stairs during the investigation. She had broken her neck and died instantly.

I started crying and told him it was my fault. I had taken Mom's lucky tourmaline. Maybe it would have protected Mom if she'd had it with her. Then I cried some more because I had forgotten to bring the gemstone with me—I'd left it on my nightstand by accident.

Dad told me it wasn't my fault.

"It was an accident. A terrible accident. Your mom

would want you to understand that, Violet. You did nothing wrong."

Even now, it's hard for me to accept that. Logically, I know he was right that I had—and have—nothing to feel guilty about, but seven years later I still can't help but wonder if my mom would still be alive if I hadn't taken her lucky black tourmaline that night.

CHAPTER TWELVE
through your incorporeal skull

Now that I'd turned in my English essay, I could get back to more pressing matters. I still had to figure out just how to finish the Logan Street investigation, and I'd told Isobel I would talk to Dirk again, too. But no matter how many times I asked him about the Black Rose painting, or what I threatened to tell his fellow jocks, Dirk kept quiet.

"You'll never find it," he insisted, trying his best to sound all scary and foreboding. "I destroyed it."

I even threatened to track down his father and share the truth of his macho jock son's true artistic sensibilities. That made Dirk pause a little, and I thought I'd gotten through, but then he clammed up. I guess he figured out that I didn't really care enough either way to go through all that effort.

Still, I wished I had more definitive news about the painting. I couldn't help thinking that if Dirk had truly destroyed it, he wouldn't be so secretive about the details of its fate.

Since he was so annoyingly unhelpful, I decided to snoop on my own. Unfortunately, there weren't that many places in the art room to stash a canvas. Isobel was right about the space between the file cabinet and the wall—it was empty, aside from a prepped, gessoed canvas, some dust, and half of a broken pencil. I checked the storage cabinets and the drying racks and anywhere a canvas could've been misplaced, but I didn't come up with anything.

At least my worthless attempts with Dirk distracted me from my issues with the locker room, which I was still doing my best to avoid. I'm not sure which possibility was more disturbing—that the thing inside was a ghost, which meant ghosts could indeed be threatening, or that it was something else entirely. The latter made me feel increasingly vulnerable; it reminded me of how much I didn't know. I could almost feel the presence in the gym itself, as if it were seeping out of the locker room and working its way inside me a little more each day. Maybe there were ways to protect myself, but who would teach me?

Then again, if my suspicions about the Logan Street house and Mom's death were correct, I couldn't very well creep in there all afraid and unsure. I had to know what I was doing.

Maybe I needed to look at the locker room differently. I needed practice, and here was an opportunity to face something that was less than friendly. If I could stand up to it and finish the investigation I'd started, that experience might be invaluable when I went looking for James Riley, Jr.

So I decided to give it one more try. Armed with Mom's protective doodads and ghost hunting equipment, I loitered near the gym one afternoon and waited for the locker room to empty out. I'd told Dad I needed to spend a few hours researching an English paper in the library; he agreed to pick me up at five, which gave me plenty of time. Half an hour after the last bell, I was able to sneak inside.

Tim came with me, but he wasn't his usual pro-spooky self at all. "I thought you decided you weren't going to worry about this. You said it wasn't a hell gate."

"It's not. But I gotta know what it is, especially if it's out to get me."

"You really don't think you should have help?" He wasn't going to stop me, and he knew it, but the fact that I was going in alone was making him nervous. It was making me a little nervous, too. Still, I wasn't about to make him go in with me again. At least I had the ability to sense this thing; he'd be going in totally unarmed.

"Who would I ask?"

"Your dad?"

"Like he'd want anything to do with this." The only person I could think of was Sabrina Brightstar, who would spout a bunch of nonsense about auras and echoes.

"But if this thing is as strong as you think . . ."

"I'm just going to sneak in and look around one more time. Maybe take a few more pictures. Try to talk to it."

Tim shifted from one foot to the other. "What if something, you know, happens?"

I handed him my cell phone. "My dad's the first number on speed dial. If something goes wrong or if you hear anything weird, call him."

Then I went in.

I suppose part of me almost hoped I'd find a bloody ritual going on in the shower alcove after all. There'd be Coach Frucile in a long black robe, standing over a scared freshman, ceremonial dagger at the ready. At least that kind of thing could be reported to the police.

But the alcove looked as empty as the rest of the locker room, and the presence was strong. Stronger than I'd felt it before. I could almost feel it pulling the fear from me in long threads, feeding on them, growing. It pulsated around me as I crept toward the locker banks, and I thought it might crush me, literally squish me like one of those booby-trapped rooms with the moving walls you see in spy movies.

And it was all drifting out from the alcove. When I

concentrated, I was sure of that. So that was where I had to focus my efforts.

I resisted the feeling as much as I could and went on. Like a cop with my gun drawn, I moved forward, darting around each row of lockers, getting closer and closer to the alcove, and the thing seemed all too happy to guide me along. I started to feel dizzy; the presence was just so horribly strong. It physically hurt now, like a headache and a slap in the face and a punch in the gut, all at the same time. If I hadn't felt it yanking me toward the alcove, I would've thought it wanted me out of there.

I knew I should leave. Just turn around and run. But I'd come too far to chicken out now.

The tourmaline. I should have it out; it should be in my hand, along with the rest of Mom's lucky charms.

Why hadn't I thought of that earlier? Before I could fumble for them, though, my messenger bag was wrenched away, the strap pulling against me and bruising my chest, before I managed to wriggle out from under it. The bag flew across the locker room and smacked against the wall near Coach Frucile's office door, and I was propelled all the way into the alcove.

Okay. I could do this. I was strong and awesome like Mom, and I could handle this.

"Who are you?" I yelled.

The shower curtains began to whip around as a

whirlwind built up in the alcove. My hair flew in my face, making it hard to see.

"Answer me!"

One by one, the showerheads turned on, blasting out hot water and filling the alcove with steam.

"The last time I was here you tried to talk to me!"

Beyond the alcove, the banks of lockers began to vibrate, the doors opening and slamming shut like they had before.

My head was muddled and swimmy. I was dizzier than ever, and I felt like my body was going numb from all the pressure. Was the alcove getting smaller? Was the floor getting closer? I couldn't think. I couldn't focus.

"You said I could do something! What did you mean? Do you need help?" I had to fight for enough breath to get the words out; I felt like I was choking. Drowning. On air.

Then someone grabbed my shoulders. I was pulled from the alcove and sent stumbling across the locker room, the grip on my shoulders loosening and letting go.

When I passed the central locker bank, its dozens of metal doors began to fling themselves open and slam shut, fluttering back and forth like loud mechanical wings. The creepy pulling sensation grabbed me again, but instead of forcing me back to the showers, this time it shoved my head into an open locker. That's when I saw the words scratched into the unfinished sheet metal interior, sloppy graffiti engraved with a knife blade or maybe the sharp point of a compass:

> Beth Chase
> Brenda Thompson
> Birch Street Badasses

The words looked unnaturally clear. They almost seemed to glow. Someone wanted me to see them, so even though I was close to fainting, I focused on those words as hard as I could.

Then a grip on my shoulders—a very flesh-and-blood grip—took hold of me, pulling me, roughly guiding me. Coach Frucile's office door was open. I was shoved inside. The constriction was gone and I could breathe again. I stayed conscious long enough to fill my lungs. Then I passed out.

Icy water splashed my face, jolting me back to something resembling consciousness.

"Addison! Wake up!" A sharp voice. Female. Coach Frucile.

For a second, I panicked. Then I realized something odd. Her tone sounded almost . . . concerned.

Another splash of water. "Addison! Can you hear me?"

"Ugh. Yeah." I sat up slightly, wiping water from my eyes while trying to relocate my sense of balance. My eyes fought to focus on the unfamiliar room.

"Are you okay? Do you need an ambulance? What the hell were you doing out there?"

"No, I think . . ." With a groan, I stood up. I had no idea what kind of story to concoct this time; I couldn't think clearly enough for excuses. But maybe I didn't need one.

"You can feel that thing out there, can't you?" Coach Frucile said. "Even when it's not acting up like that. You know it's there."

I blinked at her. "You know about it, too?"

"Are you kidding? Why do you think my office looks like this?"

Only then did I really pause and take in my new surroundings. I had never seen the inside of Coach Frucile's office before. She always kept the door closed; there was a window that looked out into the locker room, but the blinds on it were always drawn. Now I saw why. It wasn't really an office at all. It was more like a sanctuary.

The walls were hung with fabric in soft blues and greens. A small portable fountain that looked like a miniature version of a mountain stream burbled in one corner. A pair of large cushions lay on the floor. The scent of lavender—real lavender, medicinal and herbal instead of perfumey—settled lightly in the air. A prism hung in the center of the room, reflecting tiny wandering rainbows all over. A CD player on a shelf played calming, gentle meditation music. Coach Frucile even kept a tiny Zen garden on her desk. I'd been expecting . . . I don't know. A few sports posters and a weird smell, I guess.

Coach Frucile pointed me toward one of the floor cushions. She got a pair of water bottles out of a small refrigerator behind her desk; after handing one to me, she settled on the second cushion, her legs crossed like a meditating yogi.

"This is my escape from that," she said, pointing to the closed door to indicate the locker room beyond. "If I'm relaxed enough in here, I'm able to block out what's out there. Or I was able to, anyway. Lately it hasn't been working as well as it used to." She tilted her head and looked at me, and a few little frown lines appeared between her brows. "Ever since the school year began and you joined my class that thing out there's been agitated. Any idea why that is?"

I knew she was right—after all, paranormal things do tend to get more enthusiastic when I'm around, and that phenomenon only seemed to be getting worse. But how could she know that?

"You got lots of new students when the year started. Why do you think this is my fault?"

"No one else seems to notice it, for one thing. And it gets stronger when you're in the vicinity—especially if you're alone." She paused for a swig of water, but I could tell she wasn't done talking yet. "Plus, I know who you are. I know what your family used to do. Their investigation business."

"You know about Palmetto Paranormal?"

"Know about it? Once upon a time I thought about joining."

"Okay. Wait. What?" This was too weird. Maybe I was still unconscious and dreaming. "You believe in ghosts? You don't, like, have abilities, do you?"

"They're nothing like your mom's, but yeah. I can sense things sometimes. Psychic echoes, mostly. I don't know if you know what those are."

"Yeah, I know." I knew all too well, thanks to Sabrina Brightstar's big mouth. "So you knew who I was from the first day of school."

"As soon as I saw your name on my class list, I knew. I wanted to say something, but I wasn't sure how you'd feel."

"Is that why you always pick on me?"

She looked a little surprised. "I pick on you?"

"Well, yeah." I played with the label on my water bottle. "You're not usually too nice."

"I'm not overly nice to anyone, Addison. Violet. It's how I keep my students in line. Maybe I picked on you more in the beginning because I knew your name. That wasn't fair of me. But for a long time I haven't known what to think of you. You sneak out of my class. You wind up in the locker room when you don't have reason to be there. At first I thought you were just skipping."

"I wasn't."

"I realize that now. You've been having trouble with that thing." Again, she gestured toward the locker room.

"What is it? I tried doing an investigation, but all I could figure was that it's probably not a hell gate or anything. If it's a ghost, it's not like any ghost I've ever met."

"You did an investigation?"

"Sort of. I tried. So, do you know what's out there?"

"I wish I did. My first thought was that it's just one of those psychic echoes, but it's too strong for that."

"An echo of what?"

She gave me a look as if she were surprised I hadn't already figured it out. "Violet, were you happy about taking gym? Were you happy about having to use the locker room?"

"Ugh. No."

"Guess what? Almost no one is." She spread her hands. "This is hell for just about everyone, and all that misery leaves a mark. I could always feel it, which is why I have my office set up like this, to block out the worst of it. If you feel the echoes, too, I don't want to put you through any more time in the locker room after today. I'll recommend you for a student aide position for the rest of the semester."

"Will I still get credit for taking gym?"

"Yes. I'll make sure of it."

"Awesome." I didn't think the echoes were what had been bothering me so much, but I'd grab just about any excuse to get out of gym.

"Whatever this thing is," she continued, "it's much worse than just some built-up echoes. It's like it's been lying in wait. It's been festering like gas fumes, and when you showed up, it was like someone lit a match."

"Boom?"

"Boom."

Something *fwumped* against the door, and I wondered if the locker-room thing could hear us talking. It was pretty freaky, but for some reason, I felt a little less afraid than I would've been if I'd been alone, though.

"Maybe we can figure this out together," Coach Frucile said. "Do you have the results of your investigation with you?"

"I have some stuff, but it's in my bag, and that's still out there. Whatever's in the locker room pulled it away from me and threw it." As if the entity heard me and wanted to show off, the dull rapping noise bounced off the door again. *Fwump*.

"You stay here." Coach Frucile stood up and stalked to the door. She opened it, then ducked as a stray towel snapped toward her. She was gone for only a few seconds before reappearing with my messenger bag and slamming the door, shutting us off from the thing once more. "Show me what you have."

I guess I should've been terrified by that point, but strangely, I wasn't. I mean, I was nervous. My heart was still beating quickly, and my hands were shaking a little. But now that I was with someone else who knew what was going on . . .

Maybe that was the point of a team. The whole safety in numbers thing.

I handed over the notebook with the measurements I'd taken, then turned on my camera. Luckily, being tossed across the room hadn't busted it. It turned on just fine, and the photos I'd gotten were still on the memory card. I was going through them when Coach Frucile cleared her throat; when I looked over, she was holding up the notebook. She had it open to the page I'd been scribbling on the day Tim and I came up with the devil-worship idea, and there was her name, written out right next to "Lucifer." I had no idea what to say; I could feel my cheeks reddening.

She just smirked. "Don't worry about it. I've heard it before. You think you're the first student to call me the devil? The name's not demonic, though. It's Italian."

There went the Lucifer theory. Now that I'd spent a little time talking to Coach Frucile, I couldn't believe I'd ever suspected her of ritual sacrifice or anything crazy like that. She seemed pretty cool when she wasn't being an evil gym teacher.

She turned the pages until she got to the actual results. "Violet, how much do you know about paranormal investigation? How many have you been on?"

"Um, just this one. A few weeks ago. I read some stuff on the Internet about how to do them."

"Your parents never taught you?"

"I was only eight when Mom died, and Dad doesn't do that kind of thing anymore. Why?"

"You did a very good job with a lot of this," she said. "Better than I would have expected for a first-timer. But you made some beginner's mistakes."

I tried not to bristle at her words. "Like what?"

"You didn't take any baseline readings, for one thing. These EMF numbers are interesting, but without a baseline taken outside the room, you don't have much to compare them to. And you'd have to research the school's electrical system so you'd know an inflated number in one part of the room couldn't be blamed on something mundane. In this case, the wiring for the indoor scoreboard runs through the wall that separates the gym from the locker rooms. There's a lot of juice running through there, even when the scoreboard's not on, and that'll affect readings. I'm not saying your numbers aren't from the entity—they could be—but you'd have to be very careful about where and how you take readings if you want more conclusive proof."

"Oh."

"Did you take any temperature readings?"

"My thermometer went dead before I could."

"That could've been the thing out there. Or it could've been dead batteries. Did you use fresh ones?"

"Um." Now that I thought back, I couldn't remember. "This equipment was Mom's, so it's pretty old. The batteries were probably old, too."

"You always have to check that sort of thing before an investigation. Otherwise you leave yourself open to too many possible explanations."

"Oh," I said again.

She held out her hand for the camera and flipped through the photos, looking at each on the screen. "Did you use a film camera as well?"

"I don't have one."

"It's good to use one, even if it's just a disposable.

It gives you a negative to study. Digital photos can be unreliable; some investigators won't use them at all. And it looks like you used a flash with all of these; it's better to take some photos with a flash, and some without. Flashes can play tricks."

"But I got orbs." I grabbed the camera back and brought up a specific shot.

"Those look like specks of dust, unfortunately. Real paranormal orbs look more like little comets. They're moving quickly, so in photos they look like they have tails."

"What about the ectoplasmic mist in the shower alcove?"

Coach Frucile frowned at the shower photo. "It could be a mist. You're right. Or it could be high levels of humidity reflecting your flash. Did you take this in the morning?"

"During first period," I said.

"Did you know the cross-country team practices before school, then uses the showers?"

"No." Like I had any reason to pay attention to the cross-country team's schedule.

"That's why the alcove is so humid in the morning. That's the sort of thing you'd need to be aware of. A lot of your results do show possible activity, but they're too easily discounted."

"Oh," I said once more. It was getting to be my

standard reaction to everything. Then I remembered one piece of evidence that wasn't in the notebook. "I got EVP, too."

"Really? You got a recording of that thing?"

I was kind of impressed Coach Frucile knew what EVP was.

"Yeah."

I thought back to how the recording had scared me, and how I'd deleted it off my computer at first. If I was lucky, there'd still be a copy on the recorder. I took it out of my bag, switched it on, and pushed play. The sound was quieter and tinnier through the recorder than it had been on my laptop, but I could tell from Coach Frucile's face that she could still make out some of the words.

"Now that," she said, after letting it play on a loop a few times, "I can't disprove. You've got something there."

I wished I could've felt smug about showing her up on at least one detail from my investigation, but hearing the recording again had given me goose bumps.

"I don't know what it means, though. It said I could do something, but then it said no, and then it trailed off. And that part about the street—did you hear that?"

Coach Frucile played the recording a few more times, listening very closely.

"First Street," I said. "Is it telling me to go somewhere? I don't think Palmetto even has a First Street."

"It's hard to hear, but I don't think that's First Street. It almost sounds like Birch Street. There's a Birch Street downtown."

"Birch Street." Why did that sound familiar? It took a few seconds, but then I remembered the words inside the locker. "Birch Street Badasses."

Coach Frucile gave me a weird look.

"Beth Chase," I continued. "Brenda Thompson. Their names are scratched in a locker out there. Do you know them?"

"Never heard of them."

"That thing out there wanted me to know their names. Could they be students? Former students, maybe?"

"The names aren't familiar. They might've gone here before my time, though."

I felt like I was definitely on to something.

"How can we find out? Can we look through some old yearbooks?"

Though I had no idea how we could get out of Frucile's office let alone make our way to the school library with that thing out there keeping guard.

"The school's in the process of digitizing the yearbooks for an online database," Coach Frucile said, "but I don't know if it's live yet."

"Then we rely on the magic of the Internet," I said,

pointing at the computer on Coach Frucile's desk. "Can I? Is that thing online?"

She nodded, so I jumped up and sat at her desk, and pulled up a search engine. Typing in *Beth Chase* gave me pages of useless results, but narrowing it down with *Beth Chase Palmetto Crossing* or *Beth Chase Palmetto High* gave me no matches at all. So I tried Brenda instead. The first hit for *Brenda Thompson Palmetto Crossing* was an obituary from earlier in the year.

"'Brenda Ryans, formerly Brenda Thompson, 72, passed away on May 13. A lifelong resident of Palmetto Crossing, Brenda is survived by her daughter, April Ryans-Allen. Services will be held at Walker Brothers Mortuary.' Pfft, Walker Brothers," I muttered. "Those guys suck."

Coach Frucile ignored my dig at Dad's main competitor and leaned over the keyboard. "So, she'd have been in high school in the midfifties. Palmetto High was a tiny new school then. Assuming she went here."

"That makes those lockers out there older than dirt," I added. No wonder they were so crappy.

Coach Frucile just shook her head. Commandeering the computer, she brought up the school's website and tried the new database. "Looks like it might be up and running after all. Maybe we can find her if the system will let me do a search."

It only took a few minutes to find her school photo. There she was—Brenda Thompson as a high school junior, wearing a leather jacket, her dark hair swept up and back in an exaggerated pinup style Isobel might have envied. Her makeup was heavy but expertly applied; her stare was defiant.

Well, we'd obviously found the first Birch Street Badass.

"Let's see if Beth Chase is here, too." I grabbed the mouse back from Coach Frucile and flipped through the database until I found her. Beth was pretty much the blond version of Brenda in terms of attitude, although her hair was shorter and shaggier. They both looked unpleasant in their photos. I imagined them beating up other kids for their lunch money, or sneaking cigarettes in the bathroom, or whatever dumb things bullies did in the 1950s.

We flipped through the rest of the database but didn't find another mention of either of them. They hadn't belonged to any clubs or organizations; they hadn't played any sports. And they didn't show up in any of the candid photos; those photos were full of giggling girls in ponytails and dainty sweaters—the fifties versions of Cherry and the rest of the void, I bet. It didn't seem like Beth and Brenda had been too popular.

At least now we had an idea of what we might be dealing with. Finally.

"So you think it's one of them out there?" Coach Frucile asked.

"It makes more sense than anything else does. My money's on Brenda, since we don't even know if Beth is dead. Whichever one it is, though, we need to know why she's here."

"Brenda's obituary mentioned a daughter," Coach Frucile said. "Maybe she could tell us something about her mother that might give us a clue."

Normally I would've agreed, but the thing outside was still *fwumping* against the office door. Now wasn't the time to track down relatives.

"Or I could just go out there and ask Brenda myself." And then tell her to get the hell out.

Fwump. Fwump-fwump-FWUMP. Coach Frucile and I both looked at the door. "Are you sure?" she asked.

"I don't think I have a choice," I said.

"What can I do to help?"

Coach Frucile was looking to me for answers? Wow. I wished I'd had time for more research and prep, but even without that, I felt weirdly confident.

"Well, it would help if we could get rid of those psychic echoes you mentioned before. It might be easier to deal with Brenda without so much negative energy around;

it's probably getting her even more riled up." I wasn't sure how accurate that was, but it made sense. This wasn't the time to question my instincts.

"We can use sage for purification. I have a few smudge sticks I was planning to try anyway. Salt might work as well, but sage is stronger." From a storage cabinet, Coach Frucile pulled several small bundles of dried plant matter wound with red twine.

"Those are perfect." Sage had always been Mom's spiritual cleanser of choice. She'd called it the color-safe bleach of the paranormal universe, so this felt very appropriate. "I don't know if we can clear the room completely, but if we can get most of it, that should do the trick. Let's do this, you handle the sage, and I'll have a chat with whoever's out there."

I found my black tourmaline in my bag and palmed it.

Producing a lighter from her desk drawer, Coach Frucile set the first sage stick smoking. Together, we returned to the locker room.

I felt so strong, so much more confident. I had a better idea of what I was dealing with, and a new ally.

While Coach Frucile made her rounds, walking the burning sage to every corner and between the rows of lockers, I headed straight to the shower alcove, where the presence had been strongest.

This wasn't exactly like anything I'd done before, but I'd never hesitated when communicating with other kinds of spirits in the past, and I couldn't afford to do so now.

"Hey!" I said, stepping into the alcove. When the shower curtains began to whip and the water turned on and off, I squeezed the black tourmaline more tightly in my fist and refused to be afraid. "Brenda. Beth. Whoever you are. You're not welcome here anymore. It's time to move on."

Something hissed near my ear. I turned and didn't see anything, but the sound came again. It sounded familiar, like the staticky whispers I'd heard on the EVP, but now I could hear it clearly.

"You know," it purred at me. "You know we're here."

I'd been right.

"How could I not?" I said. "Look, you can cut out the theatrics. I know who you are, and I'm not scared of you."

Anger and fear constricted around me, and the tone of the whisper changed. "Get out."

"Still not doing it for me," I said, although it was getting hard to breathe again.

"Want to know . . ." the hiss said, swirling hot around my head, "what it feels like to drown?"

The words made me shiver as I remembered how the presence had twisted around me earlier, squeezing the air from my lungs, robbing me of the ability to breathe.

Then I smelled something odd and herbal, and I was aware of Coach Frucile in the alcove. She carried the sage to each individual shower stall, filling the place with wisps of pungent smoke before continuing on to the rest of the locker room. Somewhere beyond the direct rage of the presence, I felt something about the room lighten up. It was as if the lights had become just a little brighter.

The echoes were dispersing.

Brenda-or-Beth didn't like that. She gave me a shove that was like being pummeled in the chest with a dumbbell. I fell back onto my butt. Tailbone, meet tile. *Ouch*. It didn't scare me, but it did make me mad. Anger wasn't going to help in this situation, so I forced myself to calm down again.

Before I could stand up, though, something invisible zipped painfully across my cheek. I yelped and touched my face. When I looked at my fingers, they were smeared with blood.

So not cool.

"That's it," I said, getting back to my feet. "Get it through your incorporeal skull, you idiot. You were a bully back then, and you're a bully now, and it's time for this to stop." I spoke calmly, clearly, not letting my emotions control me. "Are you going to show yourself so we can talk this out like rational people, or would you rather be a coward?"

There was a flash of blue to my right. When I looked over, I saw the dark-haired girl from the yearbook photo. Brenda. Although she'd died in her seventies, her ghost still looked like her sixteen-year-old self, a mix between a greaser and a pinup girl. That was something I'd never witnessed before—a ghost appearing at an age different than the one she had been when she died. I figured it had something to do with her unfinished business, whatever that was. Yep, just another ghostly reminder that when it comes to the paranormal, there are no rules.

She glared at me. "We're not cowards."

Another girl, this one taller and blonder, dressed in a motorcycle jacket over a white shirt and jeans, appeared beside her.

"Brenda! Come on! We weren't going to do this. We had a plan."

"You must be Beth," I said. "So, what's this plan?" I looked from one Birch Street Badass to the other.

They both ignored me.

Brenda said, "She called us cowards!"

"So?" Beth said. "You see what she's like. She can hear us. She's going to make us leave. She's going to be all, 'Go into the light' or whatever, and who knows where we'll end up? We only just found each other again."

Um, excuse me, I'm standing right here, I thought. "So that makes it okay to scare me and scratch me and try to suffocate me?"

"We just want to be left alone. I thought it would make you stay away," Beth said, sounding a little sheepish.

"Why?"

"Well, you're a freak like us."

"I am my own brand of freak, thank you very much."

"You know what we mean," Beth said. "The kids you deal with might not wear sweater sets and poodle skirts—"

"And bobby socks," Brenda interrupted with a sneer at her contemporaries' fashion sense.

"Those, too," Beth said. "The kids look different now, but they're still all alike. They still don't like us outsiders. They're always giving people like us a hard time."

"People like us? You're talking like you're the ones who were bullied," I said.

"Well, yeah," Beth said, sounding a little impatient. "You think it's easy going to school in your brothers' greaser castoffs? My family couldn't afford a lot of new clothes. Brenda started wearing that jacket to take some of the heat off of me. Then we *both* got picked on."

Wait, this wasn't going the way I'd expected. "So you're not just making some questionable fashion statement?"

"No. I mean, I like the jacket and all—"

"Beth was always a tomboy," Brenda added.

"—and you'd have to kill me to get me into a skirt with a stupid poodle on it, but I dressed like this because these were the only clothes I had."

"I tried to give her some of my things," Brenda said, "but she was always too proud to accept them."

"You didn't have much, either," Beth protested. "Besides, it was no one's business what I wore. I don't know why it made those girls do what they did."

"What did they do?" I asked.

Beth didn't answer right away. She crossed her arms and stared into one of the showers, so Brenda spoke instead. "A bunch of girls cornered us in here one afternoon. They beat us up and scratched Beth's cheek pretty badly. They said some awful things, and ripped up our clothes. Then they held us under the showerheads and pulled our hair so that our faces were right in the spray."

"I couldn't breathe," Beth said softly.

"I couldn't take it anymore after that," Brenda said. "I dropped out. Beth's parents pulled her out of school."

"My family moved soon after that," Beth said. "Dad found a better job out in Arizona."

"Beth and I lost touch. We were best friends, but after everything that happened . . ."

"We wrote back and forth a few times, and that was it."

"And you both ended up back here after you died?" I asked.

Beth nodded. "I went to sleep when the anesthesia kicked in on the operating table, just before my open-heart surgery, and woke up here. That was . . . over ten years ago, I think. It can be hard to keep track. At first I was horrified to be stuck back in this room, but over time I realized I'd gotten what I wanted. I was invisible. Everyone just left me alone. Then Brenda came back earlier this year, after she died. We're finally together again. I don't want to lose that. I don't want to leave."

"Well," I said, "I'm not here to shove you into the afterlife. I really don't care where you go or what you do. I just want you to leave me alone. I know you said you're happy to be back here because you're together, but it doesn't seem like either of you are at peace. I don't know how you could be happy spending eternity in a place with so many bad memories."

"See?" Beth said to Brenda, her voice growing shrill and upset. "It's just like I said!"

"Beth panicked when you showed up," Brenda explained. "We could tell you sensed us. She doesn't want your help."

"And what do you want?" I asked Brenda.

"Well . . . I don't like being stuck here," she admitted.

"What happened here was awful, and I'm forced to think about it every time I look at those showers. I wanted to talk to you. Beth didn't. We've been fighting about it."

That explained the mixed messages I'd been getting in the locker room, the strange EVP, the alternating hot and cold spots.

"Beth wouldn't let me talk to you," Brenda said. "That's why I pushed you into the lockers. I needed you to find our names. Beth scratched them there back in 1956."

Beth said, "That's the last time we were together. What if we go, and I never see Brenda again?" Beth asked. "She's the only friend I have."

"I don't know what will happen when you move on," I said, "but I can't imagine any version of an afterlife that would split up best friends."

Beth frowned. "How do we even go, if we decide we want to? We're kind of stuck."

"Yeah. That'd be your unfinished business—which in your case is probably all that anger you're holding on to over what happened here. That's why you ended up back in the locker room after you died."

Brenda lifted her chin. "You can't blame us for being mad."

"No, I don't. But . . ." I remembered the times I'd been teased or bullied. None were nearly as bad as what had happened to Beth and Brenda, but it was hard not to let that anger stew and fester. "Here's the thing. You have every right to be mad, but at some point, you're going to have to let that go. Otherwise, you're just giving the bullies more power. It's not like they can hurt you anymore. Not unless you let them."

"But I'm so freakin' pissed!" Beth said, slamming her translucent foot against the tile floor. The shower curtains started flapping again. "Do you know how humiliating it was, being held under the showers like that? I felt like I was drowning."

"I can only imagine." Actually, I had a pretty good idea, since that was how being in the locker room had made me feel at times. "But what good is that anger doing you now? It's just keeping you here, in a place where you were always miserable."

Brenda reached out and touched Beth's arm. "She's right."

"Look, you don't have to move on into whatever afterlife there is," I said. "You'll probably want to eventually, but you don't have to go yet. I know you're scared about what might happen if you do. But wouldn't it feel better to just get out of the locker room? Maybe there's somewhere else you'd rather be. Somewhere you used to hang out? Somewhere that made you happy?"

"Birch Street Park," both girls said in unison.

"We used to live on Birch Street," Beth said, as though she didn't trust me to figure that out from the fact that they called themselves the Birch Street Badasses. "There's a park at the end of the road. We used to play there when we were little. When we got older, we still went back sometimes and sat on the swings when the weather was nice. I missed it so much when we moved."

"So let go of this crap and go there instead!" I said. It seemed like a no-brainer to me.

Having finished smudging the room, Coach Frucile returned to the alcove and handed me a smoldering bundle of sage. I held it up, waving it all around, letting the smoke curl and billow. There was a new calmness in the locker room now. The weight of the air around me disappeared. It was like the relief of a cool breeze on a hot, sticky day.

"But what if someone else gets harassed in here the way we were?" Beth asked.

"Well, we have this awful dress code," I said, pointing to my shirt. "And there are more rules to protect us now."

"That's not enough," Beth said. "I've kept an eye on things while I've been here. If I caught a girl picking on anyone in the locker room, I spooked her a little. Just enough to get her to stop. I don't want anyone else suffering here the way we did."

"Oh, but it was just fine to torture me," I muttered.

"That was different," Beth said.

Ghosts. Sheesh.

I thought for a moment, then an idea hit me. "You know, I may be able to recruit someone to keep watch here. Would that work?"

Beth and Brenda glanced at each other and nodded.

"Then I think we can go," Brenda said. "I don't want to dwell on that day anymore."

Beth reached out and clasped her hand. "It's over. Come on. Let's go to the park."

The Birch Street Badasses disappeared.

Everything was quiet and still and . . . normal.

Well, normal except for the haze of smoke that was starting to burn my eyes a little.

"Are they gone?" Coach Frucile asked.

I nodded. "We did it. No more haunted locker room."

Not gonna lie—I felt pretty freakin' proud of myself for handling the situation the way I did. Okay, so Coach Frucile helped. A little.

I had exactly three seconds to reflect on my victory before the fire alarm started shrieking, and the emergency sprinklers overhead switched on, drenching us and putting out what was left of the smudge sticks. The smoke began to dissipate, but there'd still be a lot about that moment to explain away to the authorities.

"You go," Coach Frucile said, as though she'd read my mind. "I'll take care of this."

I ran to retrieve my bag from her office, and tried not to let it get too wet from the sprinklers on my way out.

"Hey!" I called from the main doorway.

Coach Frucile was heading to her office, presumably to call the front office about the "malfunctioning" alarm.

"What?"

"That thing you said before? The office aide position? I'm totally taking you up on that."

"Fair enough!"

Oh, awesome. Not only had I just cleared out my first serious haunting, but I'd also found a legit way to get out of gym class.

The fire alarm shut off as I squelched into the hall, shoving my wet hair out of my face. It wasn't until then that I remembered Tim. He'd been out here this whole time, but there was no sign of him now. I headed to the nearest exit to look for him.

He was waiting outside, on one of the covered walkways, and he looked even paler than usual. When he saw me, he ran up and hugged me so violently that the impact knocked the sunglasses right off his head.

"Omigod! You're okay!"

"Yeah. And now you're all wet."

"I don't care. I was so freaking out when the fire alarm went off! What happened? Your face is bleeding!"

"Just a scratch. No big deal." I couldn't imagine what

I looked like—soaked through and wild-eyed with blood on my face, probably. "I'll tell you the whole story, but let's go somewhere I can dry off first. Maybe we can get up on the roof."

"Okay, but . . ." He paused, looking even more worried. "First I have something to tell you. Don't get mad, okay?" He handed back my cell, an expression of apology on his face.

"Oh God, Tim, you didn't." I checked the phone's record of outgoing calls.

"I said I was freaking out, okay? I peeked in but I didn't see you anywhere, and it was like you disappeared, and then the alarm went off, and I didn't know what else to do."

"You actually called my dad? What did you tell him?"

"Um, kind of . . . everything."

I stared at him in dismay. Then I looked up and saw Dad rushing through the central courtyard, a panicked expression on his face. He spotted me, and his expression turned to relief, followed by total anger.

Oh crap.

CHAPTER THIRTEEN
like a dead body you can't bear to bury

We drove home in silence, dropping Tim off on the way. Tim, who was always begging to be allowed to ride in the hearse, didn't even grouse about the fact that Dad arrived in his little sedan instead. The look on Dad's face made it clear he wasn't in the mood to put up with complaints.

At home, Dad told me to dry off, change my clothes, and wash my face. I blotted tenderly at the cut on my cheek; it was barely a scratch, but now that I was slightly removed from the situation, I couldn't think about the fact that a ghost had drawn my blood without shivering a little. Then I met Dad back in the kitchen. Dad wasn't usually much of a lecturer, but I could tell today would be an exception.

Tim had totally spilled the beans. He was so freaked out when the fire alarm went off that he had called Dad and started babbling about ghosts and hell gates and satanic rituals. He let it slip that I'd found Mom's equipment, and he said I'd gone missing during an investigation.

I always figured Dad would be pissed if he found out what I was doing. What I didn't realize was that it would also terrify him.

"What the hell were you thinking?" Dad paced over the faded linoleum in the tiny kitchen while I watched from a stool at the breakfast bar.

"Dad, just going near that room every morning was driving me nuts! Someone had to do something. I told you how much I hated gym!"

He ran his hands back through his mussed hair. It had always been black like mine, but now I realized how much gray had appeared at his temples. "I thought you were afraid of volleyballs, not of poltergeists in the showers!"

"I was with Coach Frucile, and I was careful!"

"You put yourself in danger, Violet! Why didn't you come to me about this? Why didn't you tell me?"

I glared. "You never want to hear about ghost stuff anymore. You just ignore it and pretend it doesn't exist."

He stroked a hand over his beard, something he always did when he was anxious. "I would've tried to help you."

"You would've told me to stay away from it and ignore it. It's what *you* do!"

"It's safer that way!"

"I can't stay totally safe for the rest of my life, Dad. Sometimes I'm going to have to take risks."

"You think I don't realize that, now that I have ghosts flinging trays at me in the embalming room? None of that happened until you came back here full-time, and the longer you're around, the worse it gets."

As soon as he said it, his mouth clamped shut like he thought he could trap his words inside. But it was too late. I steeled myself, refusing to cry while he backtracked.

"All I mean is that you need to know you can come to me if you're having trouble, no matter what kind of trouble it is."

"I bet," I muttered, staring at the scuffed floor.

"Also," he said, "I'm not happy that you went behind my back and snooped through my things."

"They weren't your things. They were Mom's, and she'd want me to have them."

"She sure as hell wouldn't want you putting yourself in danger over something like this. There were reasons she never went on investigations alone, Violet. It's not safe."

"She told me it was!"

"She lied, Violet."

I thought back to that conversation I'd had with Mom about Sabrina Brightstar.

"Yeah, well, she also told me sometimes people have reasons for lying, and it's easier to cut them some slack when you know why they did it."

"That may be so, but it doesn't change the fact that you put yourself in danger. Thank goodness your coach was there. That was just good luck. Your mother wouldn't want you doing this. She never knew what she might encounter during an investigation, and she was smart enough not to risk finding out on her own."

"What, so now I'm stupid?"

"No, of course not." Dad's tone went all weary and exasperated. "But you don't have any experience with this kind of thing."

"Because nobody will help me!"

"Is that why you've been talking to Sabrina Brightstar?"

"What? How'd you know about that?"

"Tim mentioned it."

Oh, for Pete's sake. Tim really *had* spilled everything.

"No, that's not why. And I haven't been 'talking' to her, Dad. I wanted to know if she could tell me anything about Mom, so I tracked her down and e-mailed her once. That's it. I didn't answer her because I didn't like what she had to say."

"About me?"

"Yeah." It was kind of hard to look at him just then, so I concentrated on the speckles in the gray Formica countertop. "All I wanted was to learn about Mom. Because you won't tell me anything. Not about her, not about that night." I finally glanced up. "You've been keeping Mom's stuff in a coffin. Will you *think* about that for a minute? You can't bear to look at any of it, but you can't bear to toss it, either, so you lock it up like a dead body you can't bear to bury. You've never let go of her."

"How could I?" he asked. "Your mom was the love of my life. How could I ever let her go?"

Dad sat next to me at the breakfast bar. His face was lined and tired; I had never seen him look so old, and it scared me.

"She wouldn't want you to live like this."

"But she's not here to say so. Don't you understand, Violet, everything we did—every one of those investigations—they were all for her. It was her passion, and I got pulled in because *she* was *my* passion. Before then, I'd been content thinking nothing existed beyond this world and the solid things in it. I didn't believe in an afterlife. I thought the idea of ghosts was complete nonsense. Then your mom came along and made me question that, and I went along with what she wanted because I loved her. If I'd held back, if I'd been more honest about how skeptical I was, maybe I could've dissuaded her from all those investigations. From starting the team. If I'd done that, we wouldn't have gone to Riley Island that night, and—"

"You can't do that to yourself," I said, giving his arm a squeeze.

"I do that to myself every single day. And when I see you getting involved in the same thing . . ."

"You're afraid I'll get hurt, too."

"Or worse. And there's another reason I've never wanted to talk about this stuff."

I already knew. I'd guessed long ago.

"If I just pretend you don't have these abilities, I don't have to think about the fact that you might be able to see her." He looked miserable. "Knowing she was around but not being able to see her or feel her or talk to her . . . I couldn't do it."

"She's not here, Dad. I've never seen her. She probably moved on a long time ago."

He made a weird, strangled kind of sniffling noise. It was one of those noises you never want to hear, not from your dad.

We sat in silence for a few moments. Then I found my words again.

"Why'd she lie to me?"

"She didn't want you to grow up afraid. She thought that if she told you ghosts were harmless you'd feel safe. I didn't agree with her decision, but she insisted on it. You were so little. She always said she'd explain when you were older. She thought she could protect you from anything bad until then. She thought there'd be time."

"And you didn't think this was something I should've been told at some point?" I asked, staring at him. I mean, holy crap. I'd been strolling around without a care all this time, sure that the things I saw and sensed couldn't possibly hurt me.

"You want the truth?"

"It would be nice, yeah." A little late, maybe, but nice all the same.

"I hoped you'd grow out of the whole thing. I thought all the time you spent with your aunt Thelma would encourage that."

"Yeah, well, she wasn't exactly ghost-friendly. But how could you think I'd just snap out of it, like it's a bad habit or something? Seeing ghosts isn't exactly the same thing as biting my nails."

"I know that now. But you almost never mentioned it, so I thought maybe I was right."

"I never mentioned it because you didn't want to hear about it. Neither did Aunt Thelma. No one wanted to hear about it, so I learned to keep it to myself. And now . . . now I don't know what to think, Dad. There's so much I don't know. You won't even talk about that night."

He sighed, rubbing a hand over his eyes like he had a headache. "What do you want to know?"

"Everything," I said.

"All right. The investigation was a wreck. The storm, the lightning . . . The conditions threw off my readings, and your mom wasn't having any luck getting in touch with James or Abigail Riley. Bryan lasted all of five minutes before he went skulking back to the car, and Sabrina went off by herself in one direction while your mom and I went in the other. We agreed to meet in twenty minutes in the upstairs hall, near the staircase.

"After about fifteen minutes, your mom decided the night was a bust, and she and I went to wait by the staircase. I . . . I wish I knew exactly what happened next. I was standing near your mom, less than two feet away. A flash of lightning blinded me for a second, and then I heard these . . . thumps going down the staircase. If I'd been paying better attention, maybe . . . I don't know.

"That's it, kiddo. I don't know what kind of revelation you were hoping for. Your mom fell. It was all very fast. I don't even think she had time to realize she'd fallen before she died. Sabrina saw everything from down the hall, but the lightning probably disoriented her. She thought she saw someone push your mother, and I was the only one close enough to do so.

"We called 911. The police talked to me, and to Sabrina. You know what she told them."

"So you're sure Mom just tripped?"

"Of course."

"How do you know a ghost didn't push her? I mean, I didn't have much time to learn about this stuff from her, and now you're telling me some of what she did teach me was wrong anyway. I just . . ." My voice gave out, and I couldn't explain anymore. I needed to be alone; I needed to think. I stalked to my room and slammed the door.

Great. The room was freezing, and Buster was merrily tossing a few stuffed animals around the room. Stupid oblivious pseudo-poltergeist. A stuffed pig bounced off my arm; Buster gave a playful scream and pulled my hair.

"GET OUT!" I yelled. "JUST GET THE HELL OUT!"

With a startled, hurt whine, Buster left, taking the cold with him.

It wasn't fair. I was questioning everything I thought I knew about ghosts, everything Mom had ever told me. Dad didn't want me doing anything on my own, but he wasn't offering to help me investigate, either.

I needed Mom. I needed to talk to her. I deserved that much.

I thought about the house on Riley Island. I couldn't help thinking that some of the answers I needed were in that house. Would I find the ghost of James Riley, Jr.? An echo of the night Mom died? Either way, maybe I'd be able to use what I'd learned from the locker-room investigation to help put the mystery of Mom's death to rest.

A little online research told me that psychic echoes are often strongest on the anniversary of the inciting occurrence. The Logan Street investigation had taken place on December second, which was only two weeks away. I'd have to work quickly if I was going to find a way to get to Riley Island and finish Mom's investigation.

And I was more determined than ever to do both.

CHAPTER FOURTEEN
the skeptical emerson bean

Because Coach Frucile truly loved gym, I was kind of nervous she'd change her mind and insist my physical fitness was more important than keeping her word about that student aide position. Just because we'd temporarily been allies didn't mean we were suddenly best friends forever.

Still, I hoped she'd make good on her promise, so I wore my normal uniform instead of my gym clothes to school the next morning. She took a long look at the scratch on my face, shook her head a little, and told me to report to the main office. Fifteen years' worth of school sports records—boring things like participant medical records and release forms—were being held there in a storage room, messily boxed and waiting to be scanned, digitized, and electronically filed. The job promised to be tedious, but after yesterday, I more than welcomed a little boredom. I was ready to file those papers until my fingers fell off.

The secretary showed me to a storage room full of boxes. Each box was full of old files and papers; it all seemed like a terrific fire hazard. There was a desk in one corner with a computer and a scanner; a tall boy stood nearby, painstakingly positioning a sheet of paper on the scanning bed.

"We've had another student aide working in here for a few weeks," the secretary said. "He'll show you what needs to be done." She looked toward the tall boy. "Emerson?"

"Just a minute, Ms. Aspen," the boy said.

Ms. Aspen—I'd always just thought of her as the unfriendly secretary; I'd never considered that she might actually have a name—gestured toward me.

"You've got help," she told Emerson. "Show Violet what to do." Then she left us to our filing.

When Emerson was satisfied the paper was absolutely straight, he closed the scanner and clicked something on the computer. Then he walked over, nearly tripping on a pile of papers on the way, and stuck out his hand. "I don't believe we've met. I'm Emerson Bean."

Emerson Bean . . . Of course! The guy whose name I'd erased on the guidance sign-up sheet the first day of school. He wasn't exactly puffing a pipe in his study, but the name still fit. Emerson Bean was the biggest geek I'd ever seen. Rectangular glasses balanced crookedly on his nose; his straight dark hair was slicked back from his large forehead; his regulation khakis had neat, straight creases running down the front of each leg. And now he was offering his hand like I was supposed to shake it. Does anyone under the age of twenty actually do that?

Whatever. I could be polite, especially since I'd apparently be spending first period with this guy through January.

I shook his hand. "Violet Addison."

At first he smiled. Then his eyes widened, and he blurted, "Oh! Spookygirl!" A blush spread over his lightly freckled cheeks, and he started to stammer. "I—What I meant was—"

"My reputation precedes me," I muttered. The void was apparently spreading my funeral home connection and my drawing class behavior far and wide. "Don't worry about it."

Emerson Bean cleared his throat. "Not that I believe in any of that, of course."

"Um, okay?"

"The things people say about you, I mean. That you can see ghosts. It's obviously just a rumor." He said this as though it was supposed to please me.

"And why is that?"

"Because ghosts don't exist, of course. That kind of phenomenon is scientifically impossible."

Oh, so he was one of *those*. I narrowed my eyes and brushed past him. "If you say so. Can we just get started in here?"

"Um . . ." He wavered for a moment, apparently surprised I wasn't thanking him for not buying into the rumors. He regrouped quickly enough when I started poking at the scanner, though. "I have that set up already!" he said, scurrying over. "Maybe I should be in charge of the computer, and you can go through the boxes and hand me papers to scan." While he spoke, he managed to slip himself between me and the computer. Talk about territorial! Not that I really cared. Even sifting through boxes of records and handing papers to Emerson Bean, who kept trying to chat about sci-fi TV shows that I didn't think anyone but my dad watched, was better than gym. Plus, it was one more thing to keep my mind off the fact that I hadn't gotten anywhere in my quest to help Isobel with Dirk and the oh-so-mysterious Black Rose.

Every day at lunch on the rooftop of the east building, Isobel would give me a hopeful glance. And every day I would have to answer her with a shake of my head. I couldn't bear to tell her about Dirk's insistence that the painting had been destroyed. When we could speak without being overheard, Isobel gave me other questions to ask him, things to tell him that might persuade him to be a little more forthcoming. Nothing worked.

Finally, she took me aside and muttered, "Tomorrow. Lunch. Room 314."

The next day, after apologizing to Tim for not taking him along—he was okay with it once I said I was doing a favor for Isobel, especially since the other gothlings actually talked to him now—I sneaked into the art wing at the beginning of the lunch period. Isobel was already there, waiting for me outside the closed door to room 314. She wore her hair pulled back into a bun, with only her bangs and a few long, curling tendrils left loose around her pale face.

"Is it locked?" I asked.

She gave me a mascara-heavy eye roll that clearly said, "Pfft, please," then pulled a bobby pin with a tiny silver skull on it from her hair. She rattled the end in the lock while turning the knob, and the door popped open. "So much for school security," she muttered, sliding her skeleton key back into place. We went in and locked the door behind us.

Dirk stood in the center of the room, critically studying

the fabric draping on the still life Mr. Connelly had set up for his classes that day. He looked up when the door opened; when he saw Isobel, he made a strange, strangled sound in his throat. "What is she doing here?"

"She wants to talk to you," I told him.

"Wait, he's here? He's here now?" Isobel grabbed my arm, suddenly unsure. "I mean, you're certain he's not going to go all *Poltergeist* on us, is he?"

"What'd she mean by that?" Dirk asked, looking a little insulted.

See, this was why I hated helping people communicate with dead friends or loved ones. Neither side was ever willing to shut up long enough to let me relay their words back and forth. It was the paranormal version of being a translator at the United Nations.

"Okay," I said, holding up my hands, one at Dirk and the other at Isobel. "Both of you need to shut up. We're going to keep this organized, or else I'm not helping. Isobel, Dirk's still the same Dirk you knew. He's just see-through now. He won't hurt you. Dirk, Isobel's not used to this. Give her a break."

"Where is he?" Isobel asked, looking around the room.

I pointed, indicating the spot where he stood—or rather, where he hovered an inch or so off the ground, as ghosts often did.

Isobel stepped forward. "I wish I could see him."

Dirk's expression softened as she approached. "Tell her she looks pretty with the black hair."

"All right, but I'm not here to pass a bunch of schmaltz back and forth." To Isobel, I said, "He likes the black hair."

She blushed. "I always said I was going to dye it, but I never did until . . . until after. Tell him I miss him."

"He can hear you," I reminded her.

"Oh. Of course. Dirk? I miss you."

"I miss you, too," he said. "I miss those talks we used to have here."

I relayed the message.

"Why are you still here?" she asked.

"I was happy here," he said, giving me time in between sentences to repeat his words. "When I woke up after the accident, I was like this," he said, indicating his translucent form. "I felt so alone, and all I wanted to do was go somewhere I'd been happy. As soon as I thought that, I landed here. It's not the same as it used to be, though. You don't come here anymore."

"I work in three-eighteen now. Ms. Belz lets me use the kiln, and . . . This room would make me too sad. I'm sorry, Dirk. I didn't know you were here, or I would've come back."

Dirk tried to brush his fingers over her cheek, but she

didn't seem to notice. He looked questioningly at me. "How come that didn't work? Sometimes I can move stuff. You know, make pencils roll across the floor, knock someone's drawing board over. Why can't I touch her?"

I shrugged. "I wish I could tell you. Reason and common sense don't always seem to work in your world." Or in any world, for that matter.

"Dirk, I'm so sorry," Isobel suddenly blurted. "For what I said that day. I've wished so many times that I could take it back."

"Tell her it doesn't matter," he muttered, but his face hardened again.

"Wait, wait." I raised my arms again. "I can't play paranormal translator if I don't know what I'm translating."

Okay, so I was being a tad nosy. But I was doing them a favor. The least they could do was clue me in.

I looked at Isobel. "What are you sorry for?"

"The last time I saw him here, I gave him a hard time about his dad. He'd mentioned that his dad was already researching colleges for him, and contacting reps to come watch him play. I said he should also apply to some art schools, since that was what he really wanted to do."

"And I told her she was nuts. There was no way I was going to come out and embarrass my dad like that."

Isobel didn't want to hear that. "If he was embarrassed

by your talent, that would've been his problem, not yours. You didn't even like football."

"I did! Sort of, I guess. At least people looked up to me because of it."

"Who cares if a bunch of idiots in high school think you're cool?"

"I did!"

Isobel's eyes flashed when I relayed Dirk's response. "You used to tell me you wished you could just let go of all that, ignore it and do whatever made you happy. Have you forgotten? We were going to be different together. But then, that last day, you were acting so weird about it. You kept talking about good football schools, and about not disappointing your stupid father." She looked at me and explained the rest. "After that, I told him to suck it, and I left. That was the last time I ever saw him."

"She doesn't get it," Dirk told me. "Why would I want to be a loser when I could have everybody worshipping me instead?"

"Because being worshipped doesn't always equal being happy," Isobel said.

"Maybe it did for me," Dirk said.

When she heard his response, Isobel shook her head. "It didn't. I knew you too well for that. Dirk, where's the painting?"

Dirk looked at me. "You didn't tell her?"

I addressed Isobel. "He says he destroyed it."

"I don't believe him."

Scowling, he went into detail. "It was the afternoon of our fight. I'd finished most of the painting earlier that week, but it still needed a few touch-ups, so I left it on an easel in the corner. Isobel kept telling me I should put it in the county show, but dude, my rep! How would it look if I started showing off paintings of roses? What would my dad think? I never meant for anyone else to see it. It . . . It was only for Isobel. So I said no, like I always did when she bugged me. She threatened to steal it and submit it herself under my name. That pissed me off, so after she left, I trashed the painting. I smeared more paint all over it and left it on the easel. I don't know what happened to it after that. I always figured Connelly or one of the janitors tossed it."

I summarized for Isobel, who looked hurt and spiteful. "So why's he still here, then?" she asked me. "If he was so content denying his true self and being a stupid jock, I mean. How come he's still in the art room?"

"I don't know," Dirk admitted. "Like I said, I just kind of got pulled here after the accident. I can't leave, either—I get pulled right back."

"My mom once told me there were two kinds of

ghosts," I said, wondering if that was any truer than the false information she'd given me about ghosts not being harmful. I'd just have to trust her for now. "Some hang around because they want to. They're pretty content. Maybe they're watching over a loved one, or they're waiting for someone to join them. But other ghosts are tied down by unfinished business; they can't get away. Dirk, you sound like the second kind. There's something you still need to do before you can be free."

"Be free to go where?" he asked.

"I have no idea. I guess it becomes sort of self-explanatory when the time is right. So what is it you haven't said or done yet?"

Dirk shrugged.

I sighed, puffing the hair out of my eyes. "Look. Something's made you unhappy enough to trap you here, okay? Since you're stuck in the art room, it probably has to do with art, or with Isobel."

"I'm not unhappy," he argued, looking absolutely dejected.

"Yeah, I can see you're just a big ball of joy."

"What about his other paintings?" Isobel asked. "And his sketches. Where did he keep them?"

"I didn't," Dirk said. "I trashed them all. I didn't want anyone to find them, so every time I finished one, I'd throw it into a Dumpster on my way home. Look, I don't have any 'unfinished business.' I don't know why I'm stuck here, but it's not because of that, all right?" Quickly, he vanished.

I filled Isobel in.

"He was always such a stubborn moron," she muttered. "So he trashed all his art, and now he's haunting the art room? If he secretly wanted the world to see his stuff, he sure screwed himself."

During drawing class that afternoon, my pencil point snapped. The sharpener was bolted to the wall near Mr. Connelly's desk, very close to the file cabinets. Thinking of Dirk, who never ghosted in for class that day, I stared into the space between the cabinet and the wall, where the dusty prepped canvas leaned. It would've surprised me to learn Mr. Connelly had thrown away Dirk's last painting, even if Dirk really did ruin it with a sloppy overcoat of paint. If nothing else, the art teacher would've removed the trashed canvas and stretched a new one over the wooden frame.

Something about the prepped canvas caught my eye. There was a tiny fleck of peeling paint sticking up from one corner. Whoever had gessoed the canvas hadn't done so correctly, it seemed.

But the canvas underneath was too dark to be blank.

I reached into the space and tugged at the ragged bit of peeled paint. It was stretchy and smooth and rubbery, and it pulled away from the canvas with surprising ease. I uncovered about six inches of the canvas, which was painted black and white—I couldn't make out the design, but what little I could see looked a lot like a stained-glass window without the color.

Holy crap—I'd found the Black Rose.

CHAPTER FIFTEEN
ghost-in-the-box

I pressed the loose flap of paint back into place, but I was almost too excited to sit still and bother with my drawing for the rest of the period. I couldn't wait to tell Isobel what I'd found. Could the painting possibly be salvaged?

"How's Isobel get home from school?" I hissed to Tim.

"Why?"

"I have to talk to her." I couldn't explain it to him, not yet. She deserved to know first.

"She drives. Her dad gave her his old tan Kia when she got her license over the summer."

Ooh, a tan Kia. How very goth. When I told Tim I wanted to find Isobel before she left, he agreed to help. After sixth period, we hurried out to the student lot. Tim knew where Isobel's assigned parking space was (*Stalker much?*), and we caught her just before she pulled out. She was driving Derek and Charlene home, but all

I needed to tell her was that I'd found something in the art room, and she ordered her gothlings and Tim to wait in the central courtyard while she and I ran back to room 314.

Mr. Connelly hadn't let anyone stay after that day. From down the hall, we saw him leave the room, lock the door, and go to his office. Isobel jimmied the lock again, and we crept inside.

I dragged the canvas out. It was filthy, and a trail of dust bunnies followed it, their leader snagged on the canvas's corner. Then I grabbed the paint flap and pulled again, demonstrating for Isobel what I'd discovered. This time I tore a strip diagonally across the canvas, exposing more black and white lines and angles.

"Omigod," Isobel said softly. Ignoring the grungy art room floor, she dropped to her knees beside the canvas and ran a hand over the newly exposed portion. "This is it."

She started clawing at the rest of the gloppy white overcoat, which peeled off in wide strips.

"The dolt painted acrylic over oil! They don't bond. See how the acrylic's all smooth like vinyl on the back? It can't stick to the oil paint; it peels right off."

She kept peeling and picking until the floor around her was littered with scraps of dried acrylic and the painting was entirely exposed. It still showed some hazy acrylic residue here and there, but Isobel said a proper cleaning and retouching would get rid of that.

The painting really was kind of extraordinary. I mean, I'm no art expert, but I thought the way Dirk hardened the rose's shape into harsh lines and geometric angles was really interesting. It was romantic and technical, soft and architectural at the same time.

I was so busy studying the painting that I didn't immediately notice when Isobel started to cry. Her eyeliner and mascara smeared down her face in little black rivers.

"The stupid jerk," she muttered, ignoring her tears and tracing her fingers along the edge of the canvas. "I can't believe he wanted to destroy this."

"You fixed it." Dirk's voice came from behind us, startling me. He passed by me and crouched next to Isobel. "I thought I'd ruined it."

"Acrylics over oil," I told him.

Isobel looked up at me. "He's here, isn't he?"

"He is." I watched Dirk while he looked at Isobel. "And there's something different about him."

"I can feel it," Dirk said. "It's like the world just . . ."

"Unlocked?" I suggested. He had a peace around him, a balance that hadn't been there before; he no longer looked angry or annoyed or agitated.

"Yeah, I guess so."

"You wanted Isobel to have this painting," I told him.

"I did, but I thought I'd trashed it, so I couldn't tell her. And . . . I want her to do whatever she wants with it. She can keep it, or put it in a show, or whatever. It doesn't matter as long as it makes her happy. I don't care anymore if everyone knows about me."

I told Isobel what he'd said. She beamed through her tears. "That's what I wanted to do all along, you big moron," she said to the space beside her.

"Well, do it already, you little freak," Dirk said affectionately. He reached out and tried to touch her cheek again. She gasped and raised her own hand to her face.

"She felt it that time," he said, heartened. "Why?"

I shrugged. "Like I said, the rules for ghosts don't always make sense. I guess you two are more connected now."

Suddenly Isobel looked stricken again. To me she said, "If this was his big secret, his 'unfinished business,' does that mean he'll move on now, and he won't be here anymore?"

"That's up to him. From what my mom told me, some ghosts leave right away, and others stick around."

"I'm sticking around," Dirk said quickly. He moved closer to Isobel. "As long as she promises to start working in here after school again, that is. I miss her. I promise to keep her company."

"You're not stuck here anymore, though," I pointed out. "You can go wherever she does."

"True." He nodded. "But . . . this is our room, you know?"

Isobel gladly agreed to move most of her work back to 314.

"You know, I can tell he's here," she sniffled, looking far too joyful. It was ruining her somber goth exterior. "I can almost feel him." He had his arm around her.

"I think that'll get even stronger the more time you spend together."

I promised to act as their interpreter whenever they needed me to, and then I reminded Isobel that she had two gothlings waiting for rides home (and Tim and me, too, since we'd both missed the bus).

She was reluctant to leave. "Is he sure it's okay if the painting goes in the county show? It really should be seen."

Beside her, Dirk nodded.

"Okay," Isobel said, when I communicated his agreement. "I suppose we should lug it home and—"

She was interrupted then as the door opened and Mr. Connelly stepped in. He was surprised to see us, but before he could open his mouth to question us, he spotted the painting. He clapped his hands in front of his chest. "Is that? . . . That isn't . . ."

Isobel nodded. "It's Dirk's. We just found it."

Mr. Connelly totally forgot he'd caught us trespassing

in a locked classroom, especially after Isobel said she wanted the painting submitted to the county art show under Dirk's name. Mr. Connelly offered to sign off on the submission, and to help Isobel clean off the rest of the acrylic. After the exhibition the piece would be returned to Isobel, and she could do with it as she pleased.

In the hallway, Isobel hugged me, once again shattering the illusion of her icy exterior. And heck, if she was a little morose and brooding and dramatically goth sometimes, well, maybe it wasn't entirely for show. She *had* lost the boy she loved, after all. That was reason enough for some pretty legitimate angst.

After a stop in the girls' bathroom so she could fix her face and reapply her decimated eyeliner, we fetched Tim and the gothlings from the courtyard and all piled into Isobel's little tan car. It suddenly occurred to me that this little tan car might be the key to getting my butt to Riley Island on December 2. We might need help getting into the house, too, and Isobel had a talent for picking locks.

After we dropped off Charlene and Derek, I invited Tim and Isobel over. On the way, Tim and I delivered the standard warnings about Buster; Isobel was still surprised to see the television remote floating around the living room when we got home, but after her experiences with

Dirk, it was going to take a little more than an abnormal poltergeist to faze her.

The three of us holed up in my room to discuss the Logan Street property.

"I thought your dad wasn't going to let you go," Tim said; he still felt guilty about inciting Dad's wrath the day of the locker-room investigation.

"I don't think it should be up to him. He's not the one who sees ghosts." I felt bad that I was planning to deceive Dad again, but his reluctance to help left me no choice.

Isobel looked a little uneasy at the whole idea. "So the ghost at this place is a murderer? I think I had my fill of criminal ghosts on Halloween."

"The Halloween séance was a scam," I admitted. "Charlie the murderer was really a pair of sweet old dead ladies named Irma and Delores." Quickly, I explained the scheming mechanics behind the cemetery haunting. "The evidence I have on Logan Street suggests James Riley, Jr., murdered his wife, but I think we'll be safe if a couple of us go together. Just so you both know, though, if I can't get anyone to go with me, I'll find a way to go by myself. This investigation is happening either way."

Still nervous, Isobel chewed on her bottom lip. "You shouldn't have to do that, not after what you did for me. Okay, I'll go. Just tell me what I need to do."

After our transportation arrangements were set, the

next thing I needed was Mom's equipment. Dad had taken it away, but I knew he wouldn't get rid of it. I went back to snooping whenever he wasn't around. I felt guilty; I was basically lying to him over and over for the sake of the investigation, but I couldn't just pretend that this ghost stuff didn't matter to me.

I found everything stuffed in a plastic bag in one of the locked storage cabinets in the embalming room. I transferred the equipment to my messenger bag, then arranged the plastic bag so it still looked full. A quick check with fresh batteries proved Coach Frucile's theory about the digital thermometer—it worked perfectly.

Part of me wanted to ask Coach Frucile to help. She was the only person I knew with paranormal experience who hadn't shut me down like Dad. I didn't think she'd support the idea of me taking on an investigation like Logan Street, though, and I couldn't risk the possibility that she'd spill my secret.

An Internet search led me to a local real estate company's website, which listed the Logan Street house as being for sale, unfurnished. The listing included a number of photos, and let me tell you, the place *looked* haunted. Creaky old front porch, check. Huge, staring windows, check. The rotting remains of what had once been intricate gingerbread trim, check. It even had a tower with what looked like a widow's walk. A freakin' tower! You don't see this kind of thing in modern little retirement towns very often—but I guess when you're James Riley, Sr., and you own the whole island, you can build whatever the heck you want. The main structure sprawled over a huge lot; including the tower and attic, it was three stories tall. The wood had that dingy, dirty look that begs for a pressure cleaner and a fresh coat of paint.

I found some interior photos, too—the rooms were empty except for sheets of plywood and cans of paint, the abandoned remnants of various restoration projects. That seemed like a pretty good indication that no one was living there; whoever owned it was sure to be the latest in a long line of people who thought they'd gotten a good deal on a fixer-upper. Judging by the asking price, the owners were no longer interested in flipping it for a profit and just wanted to be rid of it.

While I was on the site, I double-checked each photo for indications of paranormal activity. I spotted a few smudges and spots that could have been orbs, but after Coach Frucile's reinterpretation of my locker-room results, I didn't want to make any assumptions. Besides, the photos were all taken during the day, and the worst of the activity happened at night.

We had just one week left to finalize our plans. Isobel, Tim, and I spent each afternoon at my place, discussing, brainstorming, and planning. Buster usually stayed in my bedroom with us; we took to wearing sweatshirts or long sleeves to guard against his cold spots.

The plan was for me to bring Mom's equipment. I'd also bring her protective gemstones and split them equally among us. Isobel was going to bring her film camera so we could gather some photographic evidence that wasn't digital. And it was Tim who came up with the idea of bringing a bodyguard.

"It'd be cool to have a ghost on our side," he said, and suggested putting a leash on Buster. He was joking, but the comment made me wonder. Buster *was* pretty well trained, thanks to Mom.

"I wonder if that might be possible," I said.

Buster was in the bedroom, bouncing his squeaky burger lightly off Isobel's shoulders and squealing. Every few minutes, she grabbed the toy and tossed it across the room for him to fetch; it always came floating back to her.

"Have you ever taken him out of the house before?" she asked, chucking the burger under my bed. It came right back.

"Not on purpose. He's attached to my family, not the house. That's what makes him so weird. But if we could find a way to transport him safely and keep him contained until we need him . . . Maybe this will work?"

I pulled Mom's jewelry box from the dresser drawer and emptied its contents onto the bed. The box closed with the sort of latch that could be used to hold a lock, if desired. The latch was too small for the piece of obsidian we used to lock Buster's crate, but one of Mom's pendants—a thin obsidian crystal shard—fit perfectly. By then wrapping the pendant's chain around the shard and the latch, I could secure it in place.

"Let's try it."

I unwrapped the necklace, removed the shard, and opened the box.

"Buster," I cooed, "come here." I knew he wouldn't like the box any more than he liked his crate. But he was usually susceptible to bribery, so I added, "Who wants a cookie?"

I felt a blast of cold air as Buster approached. He made a doubtful shriek.

"Buster, we need your help," I said. "We have to see if you can get in this box, okay?"

"It's awfully small," Isobel said.

"He's a ghost. He doesn't have any physical matter. He could fit in a matchbox if he wanted to."

Buster cried out in protest; he didn't want to be locked up.

"Look, buddy," I said. "I know you don't like being confined, but this isn't a punishment. I need your help. As soon as we see if it works, I'll let you out and get you a cookie."

Buster made a whining noise that sounded suspiciously like an attempt at negotiation.

"All right," I said. "Two cookies."

With a resigned scream, Buster dove into the box. I felt it bump and shift, and I almost lost my hold on it. When the lid clattered down, I immediately put the obsidian shard in place and wrapped the chain around the latch.

"Okay, Buster," I said, putting the box down on the bed. "Try to get out."

The box shook and jerked. It levitated a few inches off the bedspread, then clunked down again. From inside, Buster wailed.

"It worked. He's stuck," Tim said.

"Then this is how we get him to Riley Island."

Quickly, I opened the box and let Buster free. He threw his hamburger at me, hitting me on the nose. I got him the cookies anyway.

I wasn't sure how much help he would be, but it seemed like a good idea to have as many elements as possible on our side. For years I had assumed it was unlikely that a ghost was to blame for Mom's death. Now that I knew she hadn't always been truthful with me, I couldn't afford to assume her death was an accident. Dad hadn't killed her. I knew that much. But maybe someone else—someone a lot harder to arrest and prosecute—had.

CHAPTER SIXTEEN
resurrecting riley island

Our cover story for December second was totally unoriginal. It was a weeknight, which complicated the situation a little. I told Dad I needed to work on a big Chemistry project with Isobel, and suggested it made more sense for me to sleep over, since we'd be up working pretty late. Never mind that Isobel and I weren't in the same science class, and that she'd already taken Chem last year—Dad didn't know that. Isobel told her parents the same story, only her big project was for physics, and she said she'd be staying at my place. Since Tim's mom worked two jobs, he was pretty sure she wouldn't even notice he was gone. Just in case, he left a note saying he was at Derek's.

Isobel picked me up at 8:30. The last thing I did before leaving was to pull Mom's copy of *Wuthering Heights* off the living room bookshelf and page through it to find her Palmetto Paranormal business card. I held the little cardstock rectangle in my hands like a sacred thing.

"Mom, I'm pretty sure you can't hear me, but just in case . . . I could really use your help tonight, okay? I'm doing this for you." Then I put the card back in its hiding place. I called a quick good-bye to Dad, who was busy in the embalming room, and ran out with my overstuffed messenger bag banging against my side.

"Got Buster?" Isobel asked.

I patted the biggest bulge in the bag. "Right here, in the box."

Then we picked up Tim and headed toward Riley Island.

On the drive, I kept an eye on the dark horizon. The evening weather report predicted a series of thunderstorms would move in from the ocean. The possibility made me uneasy because the night Mom died had also been stormy. But for now the sky was clear and starry, with no sign of lightning in the distance. If bad weather arrived, it wouldn't be until much later.

A fifteen-minute drive to the bridge was the only way on and off Riley Island, followed by another five minutes along the island's coast to Logan Street. Riley Island was a lot like Palmetto Crossing—small, neatly manicured, and full of old people. Fortunately, old people tend to go to bed early; Logan Street was deserted when we arrived at around 9:30.

Since an unfamiliar car parked in front of an empty

house might look suspicious, we parked at a small strip mall a few blocks away and walked back to the house. The stores in the mall were closing for the night, but there'd be enough employee cars in the parking lot to keep Isobel's Kia from looking out of place.

Tim grabbed the messenger bag with the equipment; I took out Buster's box and carried it separately. It wriggled and vibrated lightly in my hands; I cooed softly to him every few steps, telling Buster what a good boy he was being. We took a second to divide up Mom's charms and crystals; I took her tourmaline for myself and carefully placed it in my pocket.

The house waited, dark and brooding; it loomed above us, looking bigger in person. The peeling remains of an old paint job chipped from the porch railing, and we stepped lightly to prevent the weathered floorboards from creaking too loudly. The front door was, of course, locked. We tromped around the weed-wild yard and tried the back door. It was locked, too, but Isobel didn't seem to think that was a problem.

"I didn't want to work out front where someone might see us anyway," she said, pulling the bobby pin from her hair.

"You've got to be kidding," I said. "That might work on an old doorknob at school, but a lock like this has to be more secure."

"Not necessarily," Isobel said. "I need some light." Tim pulled out a flashlight and focused the beam on the doorknob. Isobel jiggled the pin around in the lock, listening and feeling for something. After a moment, she shook her head and slid the pin back into her bun.

"Now what?" Tim asked. "Break a window?"

"I'd like to avoid outright vandalism if possible," I said.

Isobel rolled her eyes. "Oh, ye of little faith." She dug a couple of weird-looking instruments from her purse—a bent metal rod and a skinny stick that looked like a horrific dental tool. "A torque wrench and a pick," she said. "I kind of borrowed them from my dad. He owns the apartments on Beachfront Drive, and sometimes a tenant changes the locks without telling him. He's the one who taught me how to do this."

She knelt again and wriggled the tools around in the doorknob. "I just need to work on the pins and get them to set . . ." Her voice trailed off as she concentrated on the task. It took about ten minutes and several unsuccessful attempts, but finally she turned the knob, and the door swung open. "And there you go."

"Amazing," I said, totally sincere.

I stepped inside and quickly checked around the doorway, just in case any of the more recent owners had installed a security system. Nope. We entered into a back hallway in which discolored flowered wallpaper peeled over oak baseboards. The wood floor under our feet was rough; it had probably been sanded for a refinishing that never came.

"Okay, everybody be careful and stick together. Tim, hand me the EMF reader and give Isobel the thermometer. And get out the recorders, too. We'll start with those and see if we can find where the paranormal energy is strongest."

The week before, we had pooled our money and purchased three small digital recorders. Each contained enough memory for several hours of sound, and they plugged into the computer with built-in USB ports, so retrieving the files later on would be easy. Describing our finds into the recorders would be easier than keeping track of notebooks and pens and trying to write in the dark. When Tim handed over the instruments as instructed, I gave him Buster in return.

"When are we going to let him out?" Tim asked, staring down at the box. He was less than thrilled to be the poltergeist's designated babysitter.

"I don't want to let him out at all unless something goes wrong. I don't know how well I can control him when we're not home."

Dim yellow light seeped through the windows from a nearby streetlamp, providing just enough illumination to let us move through the house without tripping on any stray renovation material. I discouraged flashlight use unless it was absolutely necessary—all we needed was for a neighbor to see a light on in one of the windows and call the police. Still, for the sake of the EMF readings I needed to know if the house had electricity. I quickly flipped a few wall switches, hoping nothing would happen. Fortunately, nothing did.

We started in the rear of the house, by the back door. Isobel and I took several readings in each room, noting our findings into the recorders. We didn't find anything out of the ordinary in the back hall or the grungy kitchen. A spare room across the hall yielded nothing interesting, either. No cold spots, no EMF spikes.

I was checking the last corner of the den when I heard Isobel go "Whoa!" in the hall. She was getting ahead of Tim and me, walking a little too fast. It made me uneasy that we weren't staying together. I hurried into the hall; Tim followed.

When I saw where Isobel was, I stopped short. She stood at the foot of the main staircase, where the heavy stairs met the scuffed, dusty floor. Exactly where my mother had died.

At first I couldn't react at all, but Isobel was nodding and gesturing, indicating that we should come over. I forced my feet to move and walked to where she stood.

There was a definite cold spot in front of the stairway. My skin went all clammy, and I shivered.

"What was that?" Tim suddenly yelped.

"What?" I looked in the direction he was pointing, through the doorway of a window-filled room that might've been a sitting room or a parlor. He looked terrified, but I didn't see anything.

"There was a shape. A dark shape! It moved!"

Even though I was about ready to freak out, I felt responsible for my friends. I didn't want Tim to be afraid because of a situation I'd dragged him into. Besides, I couldn't see or sense anything coming from the parlor.

"The shadows, Tim. Sometimes they play tricks. It might not've been—"

Beside us, Isobel screamed and jumped away from the stairs, holding her arm.

"Something grabbed me!" She whirled around to face . . . nothing. "I felt it! A hand on my arm. It squeezed really tight." She rubbed the skin on her upper arm as if she expected a bruise. "Violet, maybe we should—"

But she was interrupted as Tim fell forward with a cry. Buster's box flew from his grip and skittered across the floor of the front hall. Tim stood up, looking dazed.

"Something shoved me!"

Isobel grabbed my hand. "Violet, we need to go. This wasn't a good idea."

I nodded. "You guys go; I'll grab Buster." I darted across the room to where Buster's box quaked angrily on the unfinished wood. As I grabbed the box and shoved it into the large front pocket of my hoodie, I heard exclamations of dismay from near the front door. I turned and saw Tim yanking helplessly on the knob.

"It won't open!" Isobel said as I rejoined them.

"It's just stuck." I tried to stay calm. "Maybe whoever repainted the trim accidentally painted it shut. We'll go out the way we came in."

As I led the way back past the kitchen, I felt a hand graze my shoulder. It was like it tried to grab me and just barely missed. Nails scraped across the cotton of my hoodie.

It made me feel sick. The touch was horrible—so much worse than anything I'd felt in the locker room. The air around us went icy and stale, and a terrible sense of death and darkness rose up and drifted around us like a mist. Something hissed near my ear, something that might have been a voice. Whatever it was, it hadn't been active when we'd arrived. Our intrusion had woken it up. I glanced over my shoulder as we fled, expecting to see the translucent blue form of James Riley, Jr., but only darkness lay behind me.

In the back hall Isobel dove for the doorknob and tried to turn it. It rattled uselessly in place, refusing to move. None of us had locked it. It wasn't locked at all. It just wouldn't budge.

"Window!" Tim said, rushing toward the nearest one,

which was in the kitchen. He slid the latches, unlocking it, and tried to pull it up. The glass stayed put.

No longer caring whether we got caught, I said, "We can break it."

Tim was already looking around for something to use. In the far corner of the room he spotted a sawed-off scrap of wood left over from the house's half-done renovations. He hefted the scrap in his hand, then heaved it at the window.

When the wood was a few inches away from the glass, its arc slowed. It stopped, drifting as though caught by invisible hands—but if someone really had caught it, I couldn't see who. Then, with blinding speed, it flew back at Tim and smashed into his forehead. He crumpled.

"Tim!" Isobel yelled, falling to her knees next to him and turning him over. He blinked up at her. A thin trickle of blood seeped from a gash above his left temple, but the damage looked otherwise minimal. Isobel and I helped him to his feet.

A sudden, bitter wind picked up inside the house. It whirled and moaned around us like an ice storm, the coldness almost sharp enough to slice through flesh.

"We just want to leave!" Isobel hollered into it.

Unseen hands reached for us, grabbing and shoving. Again I felt the clutch of fingernails against my shoulder; this time they dug in until I yelped in pain. Isobel reeled back as if she'd been slapped in the face. Tim was wrenched away; the wind literally picked him up, throwing him out of the kitchen and into the hall. He bounced against the far wall and slid to the ground, dazed.

I remembered then what I'd read about the nature of the Riley Island haunting—the wrath seemed to focus more on women. This thing had tossed Tim out of the way so it could get to us. I grabbed onto Isobel, hoping we'd be a little safer together. She seemed to understand; as the freezing storm picked up around us, she clung right back onto me. Something pinched and slapped at us, pulling our hair, and a white mist rose around us, cutting us off from the world.

Through the howl of the wind, I heard Tim yelling. His voice seemed to come from far away, as though he was shouting through a canyon, but I understood one word well enough.

Buster.

I'd almost forgotten about the little box in my front pocket. The wind made it impossible to fiddle with the necklace, so I threw the entire box toward the sound of Tim's voice. Through the mist I heard him yell, "Got it!"

A horrible scream, echoing with wrath and hate and anger rang out, emanating from everywhere in the house at once. I knew that sound, and as deafening and terrible as it was, I felt tears of relief pricking my eyes. It was a louder, more pissed-off version of the cry I heard every time I threatened to punish Buster.

Instantly, the icy whirlwind and mist disappeared. I couldn't see much in the dark, but the house was filled with a series of screams and wails and brutal screeches. Some were Buster's, others were from a source I didn't recognize. Bangs and crashes resonated throughout the house; the entire structure shook on its foundation. Somewhere on the second floor, glass shattered.

"What's going on?" Isobel said as Tim ran up and grabbed our hands. It felt safer to be together.

"I think they're fighting," I said, and my explanation was punctuated by a mighty howl from Buster.

"Maybe we can get out while Buster's distracting the ghost!" Tim tried to drag us toward the back door. Isobel followed readily, but I hung back.

"I can't go without Buster. You guys go." I was worried about my poltergeist. Some of his screams were victorious and taunting, but others sounded like he was in great pain. I wondered what kind of damage two ghosts could do to each other in a situation like this. Neither could be killed, obviously, but could one somehow destroy the other? Buster had protected us without hesitation; I wasn't about to leave him behind.

Tim broke away long enough to check the door.

"Never mind," he said after giving it a few yanks. "It's still stuck."

Just then, the most horrific sound I'd ever heard rang through the hall. It was strangled and screaming . . . and it was Buster.

"No!" I yelled. I tried to run down the hall, even though I didn't know what the hell I'd be able to do for him. Isobel and Tim held me back.

The house fell silent. Not just quiet, completely dead and still. The fight was over. Tears rose in my eyes again, making my vision shimmery and unfocused.

Then the storm bounced back. Tim's hand flew from mine as he was once again thrown across the room. When he hit the far wall this time, he fell like a rag doll and didn't look up.

Something shoved me hard from behind, making me stumble forward. I lost my grip on Isobel's hand, but I could see she was being similarly propelled. It felt like a thousand hands were pushing and pulling me at the same time, forcing me down the hall.

Don't go with it, I thought, feeling strangely detached. *Do whatever you have to to fight back. Resist.* I let myself go limp and fall to the floor. Unfazed, the hands grabbed my legs and dragged me. My shirt rode up in the back, and my bare back scraped across the roughness of the unfinished wood. Ahead I could see Isobel being half dragged, half carried in the same direction, toward the stairs. She was screaming. It took me a second to realize I was screaming, too.

She was the first up the stairs, lurching up each step before slamming into the wall in the upstairs hallway, where she fell to her knees. I came second, still on my back. The edge of each step was torture on my body; I felt like one enormous bruise. I strained my neck, holding my head up to keep it from bouncing over the stairs. At the top of the staircase, I was tossed onto the ground next to Isobel. I could barely see her in the shadows, but I could hear her crying.

The second floor was freezing. Every inch of me hurt. I wanted to run. I wanted to scream, but I couldn't. I couldn't move at all. It was like I'd been tied up and anchored down. No matter how I struggled against my invisible bindings, I was stuck.

Finally I gave in and stopped fighting. I lay still.

CHAPTER SEVENTEEN
the foot of the stairs

I heard it in the distance. Thunder. The late-night storms were blowing in as predicted. What time was it? How long had I been lying there? It felt like minutes, but it could have been hours. Somewhere nearby, Isobel was still crying.

I thought of my messenger bag, which was still downstairs with Tim. I thought of Tim, of how he'd just lain there after hitting the wall. I thought of my mother and her black tourmaline. I thought of Buster, who hadn't made a sound since that last terrible scream.

It was so cold it hurt to breathe; the temperature was freezing my lungs from the inside out. My eyes were used to the darkness, and I could see my breath each time I exhaled.

The thunder rumbled again. Lightning flashed through the windows. Isobel's cries grew quiet and weak.

I was exhausted and frightened and hurting.

Outside the rain began to fall. I heard it pattering on the roof as I stared up at the ceiling. It fell hard and fast, the kind of rain that hurts like needles. The storm was moving closer. Now when lightning struck, thunder roared at the same instant, shaking the walls and floor. It was directly overhead.

The air warmed, and the weighted feeling slowly dissolved from my limbs. I flexed my arm experimentally; yep, I could move again. I sat up and looked at Isobel, who was no longer crying. The lightning ruined my night vision, but each time it flashed I could see her sitting against the wall. Her knees were tucked up to her chest, and her head was down. Her hair had come undone; it hung limp and snarled over her face. If I hadn't been terrified out of my mind, I might've made fun of her for looking like a reject from one of those Japanese horror movie remakes.

Everything downstairs was quiet. Too quiet. I wanted to hear some sound from Tim. Anything, just to know he was okay.

I turned back to Isobel. She wasn't moving.

"Isobel?" I asked quietly.

She didn't respond. She didn't even lift her head.

Fighting off the pain that tried to seize me, I scooted closer to her and put a hand on her shoulder. When she still didn't respond, I gave her a shake. Her head tilted to the side, and her body shifted and fell, sprawling and limp. Like a doll. Like a corpse.

"Isobel!" Frantically, I turned her onto her back. No resistance, no acknowledgment, no reply. Only dead weight. Her face was still; her eyes were closed. I said her name again, grabbed her by the shoulders, gave her another jostle. When she still didn't respond, I put a hand to her throat and checked for a pulse. It was there. A little weak, maybe, but there.

But I didn't have time to be relieved. Suddenly she gasped, raised her arm and wrapped her hand around my outstretched wrist, her fingers digging tightly into my skin, her long black nails pinching. Her eyes opened and focused on me.

"Isobel! Thank God." I winced and tried to pull my hand away from her neck. "Can you let go? You're hurting me."

She stared at me, her eyes narrowed. "Home wrecker."

I froze. "What?"

"Home wrecker," she repeated. "Thieving, corrupting little bitch. How dare you try to take my husband from me?"

"Isobel, it's me. Violet."

She sat up, still not letting go of my wrist. Her

nails dug deeper. Her grip was hot and burning, with a sharp, slick wetness that meant she'd drawn blood. Her face twisted, looking entirely un-Isobel-like. Which made sense, because clearly she wasn't Isobel any longer. Something else had taken hold of her. When I looked closely I could see it—a weak blue glow surrounding her. The ghost was inside of her, and Isobel was just a puppet. She stood, dragging me to my feet with her.

"My James is a weak man," she hissed in a voice lower than Isobel's. "What he did was wrong, but it wouldn't have happened if you weren't so willing." Her normally brown eyes burned blue with spectral hate.

Okay, this obviously wasn't James Riley. "Abigail?" I gasped.

"Don't feign stupidity with me," she growled. Her breath was freezing against my face.

This was all wrong. Abigail was supposed to be the victim here. Her husband had killed her, then himself, all in a violent, abusive fit, and—

And none of that had ever been proven; the Riley Island records had been destroyed in a flood before the case was resolved. All Mom had known—and all I knew from her notes—was that James and Abigail died under suspicious circumstances. No one knew the details. I assumed, as had Mom's team before me, that James was the aggressor. But what if it was the other way around?

Abigail Riley jerked me toward the staircase. I held back, digging my Chucks into the floor, trying not to let myself be dragged.

"Isobel!" I said. "I know you're in there! Push her out! Don't let her do this!"

Heedless, Abigail gave an especially strong tug and dragged me stumbling after her. She was much stronger than Isobel would have been on her own.

"I won't have you in my home," she snarled. "Not anymore. Not after what you did. You and my weak, spineless husband." She glared at me, her face a mask of betrayal and wrath. "How could you do this to me? I trusted you! Both of you!"

"I didn't do anything!" I shoved at her, trying to loosen her hold. When that didn't work, I kicked out at her legs, landing a couple of good hits. She didn't even notice.

"I trusted you, Mary!" she said again, almost sobbing.

"Mary? Who's Mary? It's me! Violet!!" If only I could snap Isobel out of it, maybe she could fight back against the thing controlling her.

As Abigail pulled me closer to the stairs, I remembered the tourmaline in my pocket. I didn't think it would do any good, but I grabbed for it anyway. My fingers closed around it; it was warm from being so close to my body. I took it out, clenching my closed fist against my chest. I wouldn't let Abigail win without a fight.

Just then another voice sounded from the foot of the stairs.

"Abigail Riley! You stop this nonsense right now! That's not Mary, and you know it!"

Abigail froze. So did I.

I knew that voice. There was no way I could've forgotten it. Its tone made my chest hitch and my stomach seize with hope.

I craned my neck to see down the stairs.

"Mom?"

CHAPTER EIGHTEEN
the other way around

There she was. Except for the blue translucence, she looked exactly as I remembered—so pretty and graceful, with her longish auburn hair pulled back in a utilitarian ponytail. She wore the same blouse and jeans she'd worn to the Logan Street investigation all those years ago.

She charged up the stairs and reached out toward Isobel. She seemed to pull the blue ghostliness right out of her; Isobel instantly let go of my wrist and fell to the ground, limp and unconscious again. I knew I should check on her, but I couldn't stop staring at Mom, standing there holding a woman by the front of her long, old-fashioned blouse. The woman's hair was a disheveled bob; her dress was dirty, her eyes wild and glaring.

"That is *enough*, Abigail," Mom barked, fully in Mom mode. "How many times have we been through this?"

Abigail ignored Mom completely. "You don't belong

here!" she seethed at me. She seemed to glow more brightly for a moment, and she twisted out of Mom's grip until she was free. Then Abigail turned toward me again.

"Get out!" She lunged forward, her rage so palpable that it crushed against me. I stumbled back to keep from falling, and she pushed again, this time at an angle, so that I had to turn. I was being herded.

Toward the stairs.

Mom tried to get to Abigail, but the woman's anger seemed to shield her from any interference.

"Violet!" Mom called. "I can't get through to her. I'm not strong enough. It has to be you!"

"But I don't know what to do!" I cried as Abigail forced me back another step.

"Just trust your gut. You can do this, sweetie. I promise!"

"How?" I couldn't look away from Abigail's snarling ghostly face. She was practically vibrating with anger.

"Abigail was sick! She had delusions. She thinks she knows what happened here, but she misunderstood. You have to reason with her!"

Reason with her? Seriously? It was one thing to try that with a grumpy but reasonably harmless ghost like Henry or two teenage girls with serious angst, and quite another to try to appease the crazy-eyed wraith, the seething fury of Abigail.

But then Mom said my name again, and I heard the helplessness in her voice. That was something I'd never, ever heard from her when she was alive. She'd always seemed so strong, so able to do anything. But now she was stuck, and she couldn't even reach out and save me.

I would have to save us both.

While I struggled against Abigail's shoves, I concentrated on putting together all the pieces I had of her story. She, not James, was the aggressor. And she'd been sick, according to Mom. Delusions. A mental illness—something that probably wouldn't have been diagnosed or treated correctly when she was alive. It had to have been terrible for her. It had to have been torture.

I remembered then how she'd attacked me when she'd possessed Isobel.

"Abigail!" I said. "Who's Mary?"

"She tried to steal my husband." Abigail's face twisted even more with hatred. "She wanted to take him from me!"

I couldn't see Mom anymore, but I felt her close to me. She spoke quietly, her voice near my ear, so that only I could hear her. "Mary was their maid. She had no interest in James, not like that. He was practically a father to her."

"Abigail," I said, "you misunderstood. No one wanted to take James from you. Mary was innocent!"

"I saw them!" Abigail said. "I saw them with that book." She pushed again, and this time when I stepped back, the ground wasn't there to meet my foot. I was at the edge of the stairs. I screamed a little and clamped both hands down on the handrail to keep from falling.

"What book?" I yelled.

It was Mom who answered. "James gave Mary a book as a birthday gift," Mom said, her voice trembling. "Mary hugged him to express her gratitude. It was innocent."

I repeated what Mom said. Then I tried to appeal to Abigail's softer side. "Abigail, you were sick. You didn't see what you thought you saw, but that wasn't your fault. You need to accept that. You need to let all of this go."

"I know what I saw," Abigail said, but for the first time, her voice faltered with a hint of doubt.

"They're all stuck here," Mom prompted. "Abigail, James, and Mary. Help her to realize that."

"Abigail, your anger is keeping you here. It's keeping James and Mary here, too. You've trapped them here with you because you won't let go of your rage."

"Stop lying!" Abigail said, and I felt her wrath growing again. "James left me long ago."

"Maybe you've just been too caught up in your own rage to realize they're here," I said.

"Call them," Mom said.

I finally pulled my gaze away from Abigail and looked around the shadowed hallway.

"James? Mary? Are you here?"

Two other blue shapes appeared down the hall. Slowly, timidly, they made themselves visible, assuming the forms of a small, balding middle-aged man, and a girl just a few years older than me. The man stood a little in front of the girl, as if to protect her, but he looked as terrified as she did.

"Look," I said to Abigail, trying to sound as strong and authoritative as possible. I didn't think she'd listen to me, but she did. She turned and stared, openmouthed and speechless.

James reached out a tentative hand. "Abby, my dear . . . Please. You've been unwell. I understand that. Mary and I both do. But we can't go on like this forever."

"But you . . . You and she . . ." Abigail sounded suddenly uncertain.

James shook his head. "We would never do such a thing. I love you, Abby. I've loved you since before this horrible sickness took control of your mind. You can be free of that now. This anger, this violence . . . It's not you. It never was."

"Please, Mrs. Riley," Mary chimed in, stepping out from behind James. "Please believe us. I would never, ever betray you."

Abigail stared at them for a long time. Then she turned back to me. "What have I done?"

"It's all right now," Mom said, reappearing beside me.

"The illness that made you think these awful things was a part of your life, but it couldn't follow you into death. What you feel now is only the echo of the anger you felt when you were alive. It doesn't exist anymore. All you need to do is let it go, and you'll see."

"But all these years . . ." Abigail put her hands to her face and sobbed. "How could I have hurt them? They must hate me!"

"I never could," James said, stepping forward. "Neither could Mary." Behind him, the girl nodded her agreement.

A change came over the three of them then. It was like the change I'd felt in Dirk after Isobel and I found the painting. They were filled with peace.

Again, James reached out for Abigail. This time she stepped forward and took his hand.

"We've been here long enough," he said, offering his other hand to Mary. She accepted it. He offered Mom and me a grateful nod, and the three of them disappeared.

Mom watched them go. Then she turned to me and said, "I'm so proud of you, I could just about burst."

Still feeling kind of dazed, I stepped up to her. I wanted to hug her. I wanted that *so bad*. But I couldn't. I could see her, but I couldn't put my arms around her.

She solved that problem, though—she hugged me instead. Even though I couldn't physically feel her arms around me, I felt her warmth and love in that hug. There was no cold spot around her, just that warmth. That joy.

But I felt something else, too. Peace. The peace that had arrived for James, Abigail, and Mary hadn't disappeared with them. It came from Mom, too, and it made me panic. I'd just found her, and now I was afraid she was going to leave.

"Mom, don't go!" I said. "Not yet."

She smiled and reached out to smooth my hair, and I could almost feel that, too.

"Shh, Violet. I'm not going anywhere. Not yet. We have time."

Tears spilled from my eyes. "I've missed you so much."

"Oh, sweetie. I've missed you, too. You've grown up. You're so tall, and so beautiful." Her voice was wistful. "It's so hard to keep track of time when you're. . . .well, when you're like this." She gestured toward herself. "I've thought of you every single day. I wondered how you were, what you were doing. You and your dad both."

I wiped at my tears. "Then why didn't you ever come see me? I waited and waited, and I tried so hard to sense you. I figured that if anyone would know you were nearby, it'd be me. But you never came."

She smiled sadly. "You don't know how badly I wanted

to. I've been stuck here with Abigail and James and Mary. They were my unfinished business—I came here with the intention of helping whoever was haunting this house, and that was Abigail. Her anger was strong enough to trap me here, too."

Deep down, I think some part of me had suspected and feared this all along. I just hadn't wanted to admit it.

Near my feet, I heard a groan.

"Omigod! Isobel!" I'd forgotten all about my friends. I ran over to Isobel, who was struggling to pull herself into a sitting position. Carefully, I helped her to her feet.

She held her hands to her head, as if she were dizzy and needed to steady herself.

"What happened?"

"Let's go find Tim, and then I'll tell you everything."

I turned to Mom. "Can you help us find Buster? I brought him here, too. I hope he's okay."

Mom nodded.

"Who are you talking to?" Isobel asked, squinting at me in the darkness.

"Let's just find Tim," I said again, ignoring her question.

I wanted to stay there with Mom, but I'd brought my friends into this mess, and I needed to make sure they were okay.

Tim was sitting where he'd fallen, leaning against the wall. He was dazed and bloody, and his eyeliner was hopelessly smeared, but he was otherwise all right. I helped him up, and the three of us sat on the staircase. While we waited for my mom, I filled them in.

"You seriously saw your mom?" Tim asked.

"Yeah. She's looking for Buster." My stomach twisted at the thought. I hoped she'd be able to find him.

"And I . . . I was, like, attacking you?" Isobel looked horrified.

"You went totally *Exorcist* on Violet," Tim informed her as though he'd been there.

"It wasn't you," I told her. "It was Abigail."

Isobel shook her head as if to clear it. "I don't even remember going up the stairs."

"That's probably for the best." I grimaced at the aches peppering my back from where the edge of each stair had bruised me, then glanced at the curved welts on my wrist from where Isobel's long nails had dug in.

A sudden squeal and a chilling gust from behind caused all three of us to jump. I recognized the screech immediately—it was a little weaker than usual, a little weary, but there was no mistaking its origin.

"Buster!" I felt like a kid in one of those lame animal movies, where the faithful lost dog comes limping over the hill at the end, and everyone's happy, and you can't help crying even though you feel like a tool. I wished I could scratch Buster behind the ears, but since he didn't have ears, I promised him lots of cookies once we got home instead.

A blue mist formed in front of us then, slowly taking on Mom's shape and appearance. "Are your friends all right?" Mom asked with typical motherly concern.

I nodded. "They're fine. And you found Buster!"

"When I realized he was here and fighting with Abigail, I called to him and gave him a place to hide. He was safe."

Tim and Isobel tried to follow my gaze, but to them it looked like I was talking to an empty space. "Is it your mom?" Tim asked quietly.

"Yeah. It's my mom." Being able to say that made something inside me swell and glow. It really *was* her, standing right there in front of me. Okay, so she was a ghost. But after seven years of missing her, a ghost was more than good enough for me.

While I relayed her words to Isobel and Tim to keep them in the loop, Mom explained more about the true history of the Logan Street house. It was all much clearer from the other side, she said, especially since she'd had years to chat with James and Mary. James Riley, Jr., was a gentle, harmless man, and he and Abigail had been happy at first. They originally hired Mary as a live-in maid, but they grew to love her like a daughter.

Over time, though, Abigail got sick. Without access to modern psychiatric treatment, she suffered as her delusions became worse and worse. She grew insanely jealous, assuming every woman who entered the house, or even passed them on the street, had an eye on James. Eventually, her jealousy extended to Mary. Abigail saw the girl as competition for James's affection.

One night, during a raging thunderstorm, Abigail confronted Mary. Abigail became violent; the two tussled, and Abigail flung Mary down the stairs. James heard the struggle; when he left his study to investigate, he found a crazed Abigail screaming horrible things down the staircase at an unmoving Mary. To Abigail, James's horrified concern for Mary was further proof of her suspicions. She rushed at James, shoving him down the stairs as well—but the force of her effort was so great that she lost her footing and went tumbling after him. James and Abigail both broke their necks on the way down and died almost instantly. Mary was only left unconscious, but eventually succumbed to head injuries five days later.

As a ghost, James witnessed the last days of Mary's suffering and was heartbroken. He vowed to protect her in death as he had been unable to in life.

"We never knew about Mary when we were

investigating," Mom said. "She had no family, and she was a servant, so her death went undocumented."

The violence of that evening tied all three of them to the house. Abigail couldn't move on until she let go of her irrational anger and acknowledged what she'd done. Mary and James couldn't leave because their fates were too intertwined with Abigail's.

In death, Abigail had directed her anger toward anyone who entered the house. She focused the worst of her harassment on women; given the strength of her wrath, I was surprised she hadn't physically injured some of the place's past owners. She'd been able to lash out so violently at Mom, shoving her down the stairs, because Mom was able to sense her. After that night, Mom had been stuck in the house, too. She spent years trying to reason with Abigail and help the three ghosts move on. Nothing worked; Abigail was too disillusioned.

"What was so different about tonight?" I asked.

"I think it's because you were here. Arguments from a ghost just don't have the same impact as those from a living person. You were fantastic back there, the way you reasoned with Abigail and got her to stop raging and listen to you."

"So in a way," I said, "I really helped you out by coming here."

"You sure did. But don't think you're getting off that easy, young lady," Mom said, making me groan. She might've been a ghost, but she was still my mom, and I could feel a scolding coming on. "What on earth were you thinking, coming here by yourselves without a proper team?"

From the remnants of broken ghost-hunting equipment littering the floor, I figured it was pretty clear why we were there.

"I wanted to finish your file for Logan Street."

"I appreciate that," Mom said, her voice softening. "But how much experience do you have with investigations? I'm sure your dad's taken you on a few, but—"

"He hasn't."

"What?" Mom frowned.

"He doesn't do that anymore. He won't even talk about ghosts . . . or about you." I raised my chin a little, happy to tattle.

"You've got to be kidding," she said. "Surely he knew I'd want him to work with you. I wasn't sure how much you could handle when you were younger, but I certainly intended for your paranormal education to continue before now. You deserved that."

"That's how I feel!"

Quickly, I told her a little more about the last seven

years—being shuttled back and forth between Dad and Aunt Thelma, being bullied into pretending the whole ghost thing wasn't true, living with Dad over the funeral home.

The more I talked, the more Mom grimaced and shook her head. "This is just ridiculous. Your father and I are going to have quite a talk about this, Violet. Honestly, I die and disappear for a few years, and I can't even trust him to make sure you're receiving a proper education. And . . . Aunt Thelma? I'm sorry, sweetie."

"Don't be too hard on him," I said quickly. "He did the best he could. Besides, how are you going to talk to him?"

"With you acting as translator, of course."

"So . . . you're coming home with me? You're not going to vanish and go, like, into the light or wherever?"

"There's not really a light," Mom said conspiratorially. "That's just a rumor. When a ghost is ready to move on, he just . . . does. But I'm not going anywhere yet. At the very least, I have to set things right with you. We've missed out on too much. There are so many things I need to tell you. You're going to be stuck with me for a while."

"Sounds perfect," I said.

I wouldn't have had it any other way.

CHAPTER NINETEEN
a tap on the nose

Before we left for home, Mom fussed over Tim and Isobel for a few minutes. She knew I was okay except for the bruises, but she thought my friends should go to the emergency room, just in case their encounters with Abigail had caused unseen damage. She was especially concerned about Tim and the possibility of a concussion, since he'd hit his head hard enough to lose consciousness and draw blood. Both of them argued otherwise; Isobel used the sleeve of her torn and ruined shirt to blot the congealing blood from Tim's forehead, proving that the cut there was minor. After helping Mom wrestle a reluctant promise from Tim that he'd see a doctor right away if he felt dizzy or sick over the next few days, I packed Buster back into his box. He was surprisingly agreeable this time, probably because Mom was there. Or maybe he'd just had a rough night and wanted to go home.

"That was ingenious," Mom said, indicating the box. "I managed to crate-train him, but I never would've thought of transporting him like that."

I beamed, extremely proud that she would compliment one of my ideas so highly.

Mom didn't ride home with us, but now that she could leave the Logan Street house, she promised she'd meet me at the apartment.

"Are you sure you can find it?" I asked.

"You'll be there, and I can always find you now," she said.

Isobel dropped off Tim, then me. In the funeral home's driveway, I offered to let her stay over. It was late, and her parents already thought she was staying at my place.

She thought about it for a second, then shook her head. "Nah. You and your parents probably have a lot to work out. If my folks ask about tonight, I'll make up some excuse. Maybe I'll tell them we had a fight and that you're a total bitch."

I grinned. "That would explain the bruising, too." She and Tim would both be making up a few excuses for their injuries.

Isobel drove away, leaving me with a bag full of equipment and a box full of Buster. As I let myself in the front door, I felt a sort of calming, pleasant breeze in the air. A blue glow materialized in the front hall as Mom appeared beside me.

"Dad's probably asleep," I said, although I wasn't sure. Funeral directors work weird hours, and since he'd had a body to tend to early that evening, he might have still been in the back, finishing up the embalming process. Just in case, I crept back past the viewing rooms and peeked in. Sure enough, the desk lamp in Dad's office was on, and although the office itself was empty, I could hear sounds coming from beyond the embalming room door. He kept a small television in there; it sounded like he'd broken out his classic *Star Trek* DVDs.

"You really live here?" Mom asked, sounding undisturbed and merely curious.

I nodded. Then I knocked on the door to the embalming room.

"Violet?" Dad called. Captain Kirk stopped making entries in his captain's log as Dad pressed pause. "Is that you? What are you doing home?"

"Yeah, it's me. Can we talk?"

"Of course. Give me just a minute," he said, his voice muffled by the door. "I'm cleaning up the chemicals."

He emerged a moment later, smelling like the strong soaps and cleansers he used to disinfect bodies. He frowned a little in concern.

"It's so late. I thought you were staying at your friend's

house. Did something . . ." He paused and trailed off. His eyes narrowed. He looked down the hall one way, then the other, glancing right through Mom without seeing her. Somehow he sensed she was there, even if he didn't realize it right away.

"Violet," he said, his voice soft with wary concern, "what's going on?"

"You can feel her, can't you?" I asked, excited. "Even though you can't see her, you can tell she's here!"

Dad was silent for a very long time. He stood, unmoving, in the doorway. Slowly he raised a hand to his forehead, as if he thought he might pass out. He looked like he wasn't even breathing.

Then, quietly, he said, "Robin?"

As it turned out, Mom and Dad didn't even need my translation services.

"I'm here," Mom answered, her voice wavering with emotion.

That was when Dad really did pass out. He sprawled back into the embalming room.

"Ack!" I jumped forward and managed to catch him before his head conked against the industrial tile floor. He was only half conscious, but I guided him into a sitting position before he could crumple again and hurt himself. He leaned against the door frame for a minute with his eyes closed. When they finally opened, they blinked rapidly a few times, as if he were trying to wake himself up. Then he focused on me.

"Dad? Are you okay?" I wondered if I should ask how many fingers I was holding up.

"I could've sworn I heard your mother's voice," he said sadly. "It was the damndest thing. Sounded just like her. Maybe I'm working too hard."

"Dad, she's here."

"Peter?" Mom asked gently, crouching beside me. "It's all right."

Still bewildered, Dad shook his head. "That can't be," he said to me, still clinging to the idea that the voice he'd heard was a delusion. "Your mom would've moved on years ago. Even if she were here, I can't hear ghosts the way she could . . . The way you can."

I remembered what had happened when I'd reunited Isobel and Dirk; there were no hard and fast rules when it came to the spirit world.

"Sometimes there are exceptions. You and Mom loved each other more than anyone else in the world. Why wouldn't you, of all people, be able to communicate with her if she's still here?"

"Because if I could, she would've come to me a long time ago."

"She wanted to, Dad, but she couldn't," I said. "She was trapped."

Looking a little pained at his reaction to her presence, Mom reached out. She tapped a translucent finger lightly against the bridge of Dad's nose. It was a sign of affection I remembered from when she was alive. Dad jumped, looking startled, and touched his nose.

"You felt that," I said. "That was her."

"Robin?" Dad looked around the hall again, his eyes searching wildly.

"I think he could see me if he really tried," Mom said to me.

Dad heard her. "I can't! Believe me, I wish I could!"

"You have to believe it's possible," I said, hardly able to believe I was about to coach him in the very subject he'd denied me for so many years. "Close your eyes and concentrate. Mom will talk. Listen to her voice. Try to sense where she is. When you know exactly where to look, slowly open your eyes."

He followed my instructions, listening intently while Mom told him how much she'd missed him, and how sorry she was for not coming back sooner. After she said she loved him, his eyes fluttered open . . . and focused on her.

"I love you, too, Robin," he whispered. His voice cracked; his eyes shimmered with tears.

With a yelp, Mom leaped forward and threw her arms around him, almost knocking him over. To my astonishment, he reached up and hugged her back, as if she were flesh and blood. They laughed and cried and kissed.

I was a little jealous that they could hug each other like that. I mean, even I wasn't able to reach out and physically hug Mom. But it made sense, I guess. Some people are just meant to be together, no matter what, and nothing can separate them completely. Not even death.

My parents were definitely soul mates. I could see it very clearly in their embrace. I could hear it in their voices as they spoke to each other in joy and disbelief.

The three of us went upstairs to the apartment's tiny living room and stayed up talking all night. Buster, now free from his box, played happily around us, tossing his squeaky burger around and dropping the temperature until Dad and I grabbed sweatshirts.

I came clean about everything Dad didn't already know—my plans to finish Mom's file, my "reborrowing" of the equipment, my trek to Riley Island with Isobel and Tim. Normally Dad would've been mad, but with Mom sitting next to him on the couch, holding his hand, he couldn't get too pissed at me. Instead, he shook his head.

"I'm sorry, Violet. I didn't realize how important this was to you. Or maybe I did realize it, but I didn't want to admit it. That was wrong of me, and it was unfair to you. It doesn't excuse some of these lies you've told, but . . ." He glanced at Mom. "I think we can look past all that just this once, as long as it doesn't become a habit."

I shook my head vigorously. "It won't. I promise."

Mom told him everything about the Logan Street property, explaining the story I had just learned about Abigail and James and poor, overlooked Mary.

"I saw everything," Mom said, referring to the night she died. "I can't tell you how horrible it was, watching you and not being able to communicate."

Dad wiped at his nose with his free hand. "It's not your fault."

"I should have been more careful that night," she said. "I knew I was probably in over my head, but I thought I could help."

Then Dad told Mom about what had gone on after her accident: the suspicion cast upon him, Sabrina Brightstar's accusations. Mom was horrified. "I have half a mind to go haunt that old bat," Mom growled. "See if I can't mess with her precious aura."

And she gave Dad a hard time for keeping me on a string between him and Aunt Thelma for so long. "You know how I've always felt about that woman. She never liked me, and she felt the same way about Violet."

"What else could I do?" Dad pleaded. "I was working and going to school at the same time, and then I was apprenticing and working here. I couldn't do it all on my own; Violet needed more than I could give her."

"She needed her dad," Mom said softly. "She needed to be assured that having these abilities didn't mean there was anything wrong with her. I'm sure Thelma provided just the opposite." She glanced at me for confirmation.

I nodded. "I used to get in trouble if I said anything about ghosts. I got tired of being grounded and not being allowed to watch TV, so I started hiding it. Dad, I really wanted to talk to you about it. I wanted you to tell me some of what you'd learned from Mom. But you never wanted to discuss it, so all I had to go on were the things I remembered Mom telling me when I was little."

"And I softened those details so much," Mom said to me. "I'm so sorry for that. I didn't want you to be scared of the things you saw and sensed when you were young. Most ghosts really are harmless, but that doesn't mean you shouldn't be careful. I always assumed I'd have plenty of time to clarify."

"You do now," Dad said. "That is . . . unless you have to . . ." He frowned, hesitant to acknowledge the possibility that she might move on.

"Violet needs me, and so do you," she told him. "And I need both of you. I'm not going anywhere. However . . ." She glanced around, her expression skeptical. "This won't do." She'd always had an eye for organization and design; she'd been the only thing standing between Dad and me and total clutter, and without her around, chaos reigned supreme. "I certainly don't mind the funeral home—far be it from me to have a prejudice against dead people—but this apartment is unacceptable. We'll need a house. A real house."

"I don't know what we can afford," Dad said, worried. "Except for Violet's college fund, I put our savings into my education and the business. I'm doing well, but I don't think I can justify a large mortgage yet, not when we already have this place."

Mom smirked. "You won't like this idea."

Dad looked even more worried.

"I happen to know of a very nice house whose present owners are highly motivated to sell. They think it's haunted, of all things. I think they'd entertain just about any offer. The place needs some work, but with a little time and effort, it'd be a fine home and a good long-term investment."

Dad stared at her. "You don't mean the Logan Street property. You can't."

Mom shrugged. "Riley Island's only ten miles away. It wouldn't be much of a commute. Maybe you could even open a branch there eventually. And I believe it's in the same school zone, so Violet wouldn't need to change schools again."

"How could you expect me—us—to live there?" Dad asked, indicating himself and me. "To live in the house where you died?" He looked stricken at the thought. I didn't blame him for freaking out a little. Mom's suggestion was making me kind of nervous, too.

"Because I'd be there with you," she said. "We'd be together. It's a beautiful house, Peter. I should know. I was stuck there for seven years."

"So why would you want to go back?" I asked.

"It's changed now," she said. "Abigail and the others are gone. It's clean and empty and waiting, and we could make it into a real home."

"I don't know if I could ever think of it as anything other than the place where you died," Dad said, sounding slightly desperate.

"Really, Peter. You make that sound so *final*." Mom shook her head. "I'm back, aren't I? You were always the practical one. It's just a house." She looked back at me. "Don't you worry. I'll convince him. Persuading your father was always one of my specialties."

"What about the psychic echoes?" I asked. "There've got to be some strong ones."

"We'll cleanse the house, Violet. You and me. We'll get rid of all that. A few old echoes can't stand up to the new life we can give it." She looked at Dad. "Peter, please consider it. I heard the owners talking the last time they visited. Abigail started pestering them, and they were terrified. They can't wait to get rid of it."

"I don't know," he said, still sounding disturbed.

Mom continued. "Then you could rent the apartment to an apprentice or an assistant. It looks like you're busy enough to need some help."

Dad scratched his head. "I have been meaning to look for someone. And . . . I suppose I could look into expanding on Riley Island. Maybe have a little office and showroom there."

Mom nodded as if the decision was made and the contracts were already signed. "We'll tour the Logan Street house tomorrow."

I looked out the window. The sky was a hazy gray with a stripe of rose near the horizon.

"It's already tomorrow."

CHAPTER TWENTY
riley island paranormal

A week later, Dad signed the last of the contracts on the Logan Street house. The owners agreed to an insanely low offer, and the closing was to take place almost immediately. The house would be ours before the new year. The owners were so glad to be rid of the property, they even allowed us to start fixing up the place while we waited for everything to be finalized. Mom was delighted; she was already making plans and merrily bossing us around the hardware store while we bought supplies for the most pressing repairs. Dad was still pretty weirded out by the whole thing, but he was slowly getting used to the idea.

I thought I'd feel really weird about the house, too, but it seemed completely different in the daylight, especially now that it was ghost-free (except for Mom, of course). It felt welcoming and open, as though it had been waiting a long time for the right residents. One of the first things I did was to cleanse the place with sage smudge sticks, under Mom's guidance. After that, I never noticed any creepy echoes, and it really did feel like our home.

It felt so natural having Mom back, even if she wasn't exactly your typical mom anymore. Moving in to the place responsible for a family member's death wasn't typical, either . . . but we weren't exactly a typical family, now were we?

Mom was right about the school zones, too—I was relieved that I could still go to Palmetto High after the move. I had friends now, and I didn't want to leave them. If I had to put up with occasional sneers from the void and being called "Spookygirl" now and then, I could deal. I even kind of liked it. It was sort of fun knowing stupid people were scared of me.

As for the rest of the school, it was as haunted as ever. I'd hoped that sending Delores on the warpath would rid me of grumpy old Henry. Naturally, he'd refused to budge, which left me with two ghosts aimlessly wandering the halls instead of just one. But what at first seemed like a pain in the butt turned out to be the perfect way to honor Beth and Brenda's request. I now had Delores monitoring things in the girls' locker room, and Henry watching over the boys'. Anything they saw would be reported to me, and I'd report it to Coach Frucile. Henry was happy to be useful again, since he wasn't much good with a mop anymore. Plus, it gave Delores an excuse to be gossipy and nosy, which kept her out of Henry's unkempt hair.

I still spent some afternoons helping Dad at the funeral home, but on other days I took the Riley Island bus to our new house instead. Since Mom wasn't much use with a hammer or paintbrush, I did what I could under her supervision.

Dad gave word to a couple of his old professors that he was looking for an apprentice or assistant, and they recommended some of their interested students. The apartment was a big draw for the younger, unattached candidates. Dad scheduled a bunch of interviews for January, and he was hopeful he'd find someone great for the job.

In fact, life would've been just about perfect if it weren't for the fact that Dad refused to consider resurrecting Palmetto Paranormal. He wouldn't even listen to my many, many arguments in favor of it, especially after I'd come so close to getting maimed or mangled or worse the night I found Mom. She promised to work on him, though, and I knew she'd succeed eventually. In the meantime, I fully intended to sneak in a little more unsupervised practice.

Either way, it was awesome having Mom around again. On the days I spent helping with home repairs,

I'd get off the bus and walk down to our house on Logan Street, and she'd be there waiting for me.

One afternoon just before winter break, I arrived home to a delighted screech and a burst of freezing wind that nearly knocked me over. Now that Mom was back, Buster seemed even more excitable than ever.

Mom appeared at the bottom of the stairs, shaking her head.

"Buster!" she scolded. "Don't make me use the crate." She smiled at me. "How was school, sweetie?"

"It was fine. Hey, I got an A on my midterm English essay."

Okay, so I'd more than gotten an A. My essay had made Ms. Geller weep in front of the whole class. Not that I'm bragging or anything, but you know . . .

I didn't get the chance to tell Mom the details, though, because just then a car horn beeped in the driveway. I looked out and saw Tim and Isobel beckoning to me from Isobel's car. I told Mom I'd be out for a while, then grabbed my bag, ran out, and jumped in the backseat.

They wouldn't tell me what was going on until we got to Isobel's place and went up to her room. Then they each handed me a small box wrapped in purple paper with shiny black ribbons. The gift tags had tiny skulls wearing Santa hats—I recognized Isobel's drawing style immediately.

"You guys!" I said, feeling sheepish. "I haven't gotten

around to buying your presents yet." Who had time for Christmas shopping in between midterms and death spackle and repainting the front porch?

"Like we care? Open mine first," Tim said.

I did as instructed. Inside the box was an odd little pendant on a purple cord. The pendant looked like a tiny mishmash of silver wire; Tim snatched it back and asked if I had my mom's black tourmaline with me.

"Of course." I pulled it from my pocket. "I always have it."

"And now it'll be easier to keep it with you." He took the stone and pressed it into the pendant; the wire wrapped around it, caging it perfectly. "I used some of my chain-mail stuff to make this."

"Omigod!" I grabbed it back and examined it, then slipped the cord over my head. It was so cool. Wearing the tourmaline around my neck made it feel even closer and more precious.

"Now mine!" Isobel said, grinning more widely than any self-respecting Queen of the Goths should ever grin.

I tore into her present. Inside the wrapping was a rectangular cardboard box just a few inches wide, and inside the box were . . . business cards.

The most badass business cards I'd ever seen.

They were purple, of course, with a purple-and-black striped border, a few striking white accents, and a tiny bat logo. RILEY ISLAND PARANORMAL was spelled out in a sophisticated black font across the top. Below that it said VIOLET ADDISON—LEAD PARANORMAL INVESTIGATOR.

Nice.

"I only got a few printed," Isobel said, "so we can change whatever you want. We can change the whole design. After you came up with the team name last week, I just couldn't resist designing a mock-up for you."

I blinked a few times, forcing back the tears pricking my eyes at the memory of Mom's plain white Palmetto Paranormal business card. This was exactly what I'd wanted.

"It's perfect. It's really perfect."

"Really? Awesome." Isobel beamed.

Riley Island Paranormal. RIP. Seriously, could it get any better?

"I got some made for Tim and me as well," Isobel said. "We're just investigators, though. You're the leader."

I wasn't sure how my parents would feel about that, but I liked it. Isobel went into a whole speech after that, about how she'd done other versions of the logo and could put together a website as soon as we were officially up and running. I only half heard her; I was too busy staring at the card. It felt so right, and it looked so good.

"Now all we need are some ghosts to investigate,"

Isobel said when she was done pitching her various plans for RIP. "Has your dad agreed to supervise the team yet?"

"No, but I'm sure he'll change his mind soon."

"In the meantime," Tim said, pulling some papers from his backpack, "I found a few reports online of supposed Riley Island hauntings. Nothing big, just some silly stuff—a pet store downtown that the owner says is haunted by the ghost of his prize bulldog, and a bakery where the late pastry chef still shows up at three every morning and turns on the ovens. Stuff like that. But I thought maybe . . ."

"Hey, we gotta start somewhere, right?"

I thought of Mama Chen's back in Palmetto Crossing; there were probably plenty of other places like that in the surrounding towns as well. We could start small, get some practice, and then move on to more interesting cases once Dad realized this was happening with or without his approval.

Riley Island Paranormal was officially in business. After all, we had business cards. We had equipment. We were a team. What else did we need?

Acknowledgments

First and foremost: Mom and Dad. Thank you for your endless support and encouragement, and for believing this would happen even when I didn't. Thank you for warping my mind so wonderfully with *Ghostbusters* and the Haunted Mansion when I was four. "Thank you" really can't cover it, no matter how many times I say or write those words. And thanks, Jesse, for . . . Well, you haven't read the book yet, but that's okay. You're still a fantastic brother.

Thank you to Amazon, Penguin Group (USA), and CreateSpace for sponsoring the Amazon Breakthrough Novel Award and giving me this opportunity. (And thank you to Thom Kephart of Amazon for all you did to coordinate the awards' weekend in Seattle!)

A huge thank you to Julie Strauss-Gabel and Liza Kaplan of Dutton Children's Books for all you've done to help me debut Violet at her most awesome. Your enthusiasm has been nothing short of amazing. Thank you for connecting so strongly with my spooky little girl.

Dava Butler, thank you for the balance you inspire in my paranormalcy—you are the Harold Ramis to my Dan Aykroyd, the Egon to my Ray. You are awesomesocks.

Rhonda Jones, thank you for being the other half of my writers' support group, and for getting me out of my crate. And for the wine. Mustn't forget the wine.

Elizabeth Vitale, thank you for introducing me to the delightfully grotty concept of eye caps!

Chrissy Skinner, thank you for creating Violet's first fan-art!

Thank you so much to everyone else who read drafts or excerpts along the way: Susan, Linnie, Laura, Heather, Lara, Shelley, Christina, Danielle, Katrina, Melonie, Denise, and the rest. Your feedback was so helpful, your support immeasurably appreciated.

Thank you, Tiny and Slippers, for keeping me company while I revised.

Ginormous thanks to Team Spookygirl for your support during the ABNA finals: the folks at Rookies Bar & Grill, North Naples Dialysis, the Marco office of Coldwell Banker Residential Real Estate, my Mint Conspiracy peeps, all you New Jersey Baguchinskys, and everyone who read, reviewed, voted, and spread the word. Extra thanks to Alan Byard, who pre-ordered before I knew the book was for sale!

Finally, what kind of writer would I be if I didn't acknowledge my favorite muse? You know who you are, you big Irish grump. I love you fiercely.